WE DO NOT PART

WE DO NOT PART

Han Kang

Translated by
e. yaewon & Paige Aniyah Morris

HAMISH HAMILTON
an imprint of
PENGUIN BOOKS

HAMISH HAMILTON

UK | USA | Canada | Ireland | Australia
India | New Zealand | South Africa

Hamish Hamilton is part of the Penguin Random House group of companies
whose addresses can be found at global.penguinrandomhouse.com.

Penguin Random House UK,
One Embassy Gardens, 8 Viaduct Gardens, London SW11 7BW

penguin.co.uk
global.penguinrandomhouse.com

Penguin
Random House
UK

First published 2025

001

This book is published with the support of the Literature
Translation Institute of Korea (LTI Korea)

Typeset by Jouve (UK), Milton Keynes
Printed and bound in Great Britain by Clays Ltd, Elcograf S.p.A.

The authorized representative in the EEA is Penguin Random House Ireland,
Morrison Chambers, 32 Nassau Street, Dublin D02 YH68

A CIP catalogue record for this book is available from the British Library

ISBN: 978-0-241-60026-9

Contents

PART ONE

Bird

I

Crystals

A sparse snow was falling.

I stood on flat land that edged up a low hill. Along the brow of this hill and down its visible face to the seam of the plain, thousands of black tree trunks jutted from the earth. They varied in height, like a crowd of people ranging in age, and were about as thick as railway sleepers, though nowhere near as straight. Stooped and listing, they gave the impression of a thousand men, women and haggard children huddling in the snow.

Was this a graveyard? I wondered. Are these gravestones?

I walked past the torsos – treetops lopped off, exposed cross sections stippled with snowflakes that resembled salt crystals; I passed the prostrating barrows behind them. My feet stilled as I noticed the sensation of water underfoot. That's strange, I thought. Within moments the water was up to my ankles. I looked back. What I saw astonished me: the far horizon turned out to be the shoreline. And the sea was crashing in.

The words tumbled from my lips: Who would bury people in such a place?

The current was strong. Had the tide surged in and out like this each day? Were the lower mounds hollowed out, the bones long since swept away?

There was no time. The graves already underwater were out of reach, but the remains higher up the slope, I needed to move them to safety. Now, before the sea encroached further. But how? There was no one around. I had no shovel. How would I get to them all? At a loss, I ran through the thicket of black trees, knees cleaving the rising water.

When I opened my eyes, the day had yet to break. The snowy field, the black torsos, the flood tide were gone; the only thing that met my stare was the window of my darkened room. I shut my eyes. Another dream about G—, it had to be. At this thought, I covered my lids with the cold palm of my hand and lay there unmoving.

The dream had come to me in the summer of 2014, a couple of months after the publication of my book about the massacre in G——. Over the next four years, it had never occurred to me to question the dream's connection to that city. But this summer I began to wonder if there might be something more to it. If my quick, intuitive conclusion had either been in error or an oversimplification.

The sweltering night heat hadn't let up for three weeks. Once again, I was lying under the broken air conditioner in my sitting room, hoping for sleep. I'd already taken several cold showers, but though I lay on the bare floor, my sweat-drenched body wouldn't cool. Finally, around five in the morning, the temperature began to drop. It was to be a brief grace, as the sun would be up in another half-hour. But I felt I might sleep at last, and had in fact nearly drifted off, when the plain rolled in beneath my closed lids: snow scattering over rows of black timber; glimmering snowflakes studding the severed torsos like salt; all of it before my eyes, as vivid as day.

I don't know what set it off, the shaking. My body seemed to be racked by sobs, though my eyes remained dry. Was this terror? Or anxiety, agitation, perhaps an abrupt anguish? No, it was a bone-chilling awareness. That a giant, invisible knife – the weight of its heavy blade beyond any human capacity to wield it – hung in the air, with me as its target. As I lay pinned and staring.

The black-blue sea billowing in to dredge the bones away from beneath the mounds – it occurred to me for the first time that this might not be an allusion to the massacred people and the decades that followed. It could simply be a personal omen. Yes, perhaps that landscape of flooded graves and silent headstones was an intimation brought forward in time, a sign of what remained of my life to come.

This very moment, in other words.

In the four years between the first time I had the dream and that early summer morning, I had parted ways with several people in my life. Some of these partings had been by choice, while others had caught me entirely unawares; I'd fought the latter with everything I had. If, as various ancient faiths say, there exists in a celestial realm or a netherworld an immense mirror that observes and logs everyone's movements, I'm sure the last three to four years of my life as recorded there must resemble a snail coming out of its shell to push along a knife's edge. A body desiring to live. A body pricked and nicked. A body spurning, embracing, clinging. A body kneeling. A body entreating. A body seeping blood or pus or tears.

Then in late spring of this year, with the struggle done, I had signed the lease on a flat in an open-corridor apartment complex just outside Seoul. I had no one left to take care of and no job to get to, though it would take a while for this fact to sink in. I'd worked for many years to make a living and support my family. This had always been the priority. If I wrote at all, it was by cutting back on sleep while nursing a secret hope that one day I'd be given as much time as I desired to write. But by spring any such longing had vanished.

I let my things lie wherever the movers had blithely unpacked them, and spent most of my time in bed, though I barely slept. This went on until July. I didn't cook. I didn't venture outside. I subsisted on water and small quantities of rice and white kimchi that I ordered online and had delivered, and when the migraines and abdominal spasms hit, I vomited up what I had eaten. I'd already sat down one night and written out a will. In a letter that simply began *Please see to the following*, I had briefly noted which box in which drawer held my bank books, certificate of insurance and lease agreement, how much of my money I wished to be spent to what end, and to whom the rest of my savings should be delivered. As for the person who was to carry out this request, I drew a blank, and the space where the name of the recipient should go remained empty. I couldn't decide who, if anyone, deserved such an imposition. I tried adding a word or two of thanks and apology by saying I'd make sure to compensate them for their trouble and specifying an amount, but I still couldn't settle on a name.

What finally roused me out of the mire of my bed, after weeks of struggling to sleep, was my sense of responsibility towards this unidentified recipient. Calling to mind my few acquaintances, one of whom, though the exact person was yet to be determined, would be left to deal with any loose ends, I started putting the flat in order. The rows of empty water bottles in the kitchen, the

clothing and blankets that were sure to be a nuisance, any personal records, diaries and notes had
to be discarded. With the initial bundles of trash
in each hand, I slipped on a pair of trainers and
opened the front door for the first time in two
months. The summer sun flooded the west-facing
corridor; the afternoon light was a revelation. I
rode the lift down, passed by the guard's room,
crossed the compound square – and felt, all the
while, that I was witnessing something. The
lived-in world. The day's weather. The humidity
in the air and the pull of gravity.

Returning upstairs, I walked past the mounds
of fabric and into the bathroom. I turned the hot
water on and sat under the shower fully dressed.
The tiles beneath my curled feet, the steam gradually making it hard to breathe, the cotton shirt
growing heavy as it plastered against my back,
the water sluicing down my forehead, and the
hair which by now covered my eyes to my chin,
chest, stomach: I can feel each and every sensation still.

I walked out of the bathroom, peeled off my
sodden outfit, rummaged around and put on what
decent clothes I could find. I folded two 10,000-
won notes into little squares, slipped them into

my pocket and went outside. I walked to a juk shop behind a nearby subway station and ordered what seemed the mildest item on their menu, a pine-nut juk. I took my time with the unduly hot bowl of rice porridge and, as I did, people walked past the window in bodies that looked fragile enough to shatter. Life was exceedingly vulnerable, I realized. The flesh, organs, bones, breaths passing before my eyes all held within them the potential to snap, to cease – so easily, and by a single decision.

That is how death avoided me. Like an asteroid thought to be on a collision course avoids Earth by a hair's breadth, hurtling past at a furious velocity that knows neither regret nor hesitation.

～

I had not reconciled with life, but I had to resume living.

Close to two months of seclusion and near-starvation had left me with considerable muscle loss. To break the cycle of migraines, stomach spasms and caffeine-rich painkillers, I needed to eat and move with regularity. But before I could attempt anything in earnest, the heatwave set in. On the first day the mercury climbed past our average body temperature, I turned on the air conditioner the previous tenant had left behind, only to discover it was broken. When my calls to various AC repair companies finally got through, I was invariably told that they were inundated with requests at the moment due to the extreme weather and the earliest anyone could pay a visit was in late August. Buying a new AC unit wasn't any easier.

The wise thing would have been to seek shelter in cool indoor spaces. But I couldn't face being around other people in cafés or libraries or banks. So I did what I could: lie plastered on the sitting-room floor and try to keep my body temperature down, take frequent cold-water showers to prevent heat exhaustion, and venture outside for some juk around eight o'clock when the swelter had dissipated somewhat. The shop's conditioned air was incredibly pleasant, while outside, past the windows that were as steamed up as on a winter's night, people surged forward, each clutching a portable fan aimed at their face as they headed home for the night. Filling the tropical-night streets whose heat, like eternity, wouldn't let up, and which in due time I would have to re-enter.

On one of those nights, I walked out of the shop and stopped at a crossing, where I felt a rush of hot air on my face from the still-warm asphalt. I had to resume my letter, I thought. No, I had to start afresh. I would write a new note to replace the missive addressed to no one, the one I'd slipped into an envelope marked 'Last Will' in permanent ink. I would start from scratch. I would change tack.

But to write it, I first had to think.

When had everything begun to fall apart?
Where was the fork in the road?
Which rift and which break had been the tipping point?

There are people who brandish their sharpest weapon as they are taking their leave. We know this from experience. They do this so as to slice the tenderest part of the person they are leaving with the precision that proximity grants us.

I don't want to live face down on the ground like you.

I'm leaving you so I can breathe.
  I want to live, not be half-dead.

~

I started having nightmares in the winter of 2012, after I began researching the book I went on to write. Initially these were dreams of outright violence. Running from airborne troops, being bludgeoned on the shoulder, falling to the ground. I can't recall the face of the uniformed man who kicked me in the flank as I lay sprawled on the ground and turned me over with his boots. What I do remember is the shudder that ran through me when he grabbed his gun with both hands and pushed the bayonet into my chest.

Not wanting to cast a gloom over my family — my daughter, especially — I found a writing space a fifteen-minute walk away from home. The plan was to limit my writing to that place and to return to daily life the moment I left it. The room was on the first floor of a brick house that had been built in the 1980s and hadn't seen any repairs in three decades. I bought a tin of white water-based paint and daubed it over the heavily scratched metal door, then I hung a scarf above the room's window to obscure the crack in the old wooden frame. From nine in the morning until noon on the days when I had classes to teach, and until five o'clock on the days when I didn't, I went there to read materials I'd gathered or to make notes.

In the mornings and evenings, I continued to cook meals and sit down to eat with my family. I tried to have as many conversations as I could with my daughter, who had just started middle school and was encountering new situations at every turn. But I felt split in half. Even within those private moments, I could sense the shadow of the book lurking – when I turned on the gas ring and waited for the water in the pot to boil, or in the brief time it took to dredge tofu slices in egg wash and watch them crisp up on both sides.

The writing space was reached by a path running along a stream, and there was a section where the heavily tree-lined path sloped down before suddenly opening up. I had to walk across that exposed tract of land for about three hundred metres to reach the empty lot under the bridge that doubled as a roller rink. This distance seemed insurmountable, for while I skittered over it, I was entirely vulnerable and defenceless. I imagined snipers lying in wait on the rooftops flanking the single-lane road opposite, rifles aimed at the people below. I knew of course that this was nonsensical, that it was only my anxiety talking.

One night in late spring of 2013, as my insomnia worsened and my breathing became increasingly shallow — 'Why must you breathe like that?' my daughter had complained to me one day — I was startled awake around one o'clock from a nightmare. Giving up on sleep altogether, I went outside to buy some water. There wasn't anyone about, not even a passing car, which made the traffic lights seem redundant. But I stood and waited for the signal to turn green, my mind drifting as I gazed at the blazing twenty-four-hour convenience store on the other side of the two-lane road that led to the apartment complex. When I refocused, there was a line of about thirty men walking single file along the opposite pavement. Their hair was long, they were in

reserve-forces uniform, and though each carried
a shoulder rifle, they dawdled like tired children
on a school excursion, their feet dragging and
their postures slack and undisciplined.

When someone who hasn't slept soundly in a
while, who is stumbling through a period of
nightmares blurring with reality, chances across a
scene that defies belief, they may well initially
doubt themselves. Am I actually seeing this?
Surely this must be part of my nightmare? And:
How much can I trust my own senses?

The men were enveloped in a hushed silence,
as though someone had hit the mute button on
the scene unfolding before me. I remained still,
following their backs with my eyes until the last
one disappeared round the murky crossroads. It
wasn't a dream. I wasn't the least bit drowsy
and I hadn't been drinking. But neither could I
quite believe what I'd seen. I told myself the
men may be out on night training, as after all
there was a reserve-forces training area in
Naegok-dong, just past Umyeonsan. However,
that would imply that the men had marched a
dozen kilometres over the hill at this late hour
and in the pitch dark. Whether this was com-
mensurate training for a reserve troop, I didn't

know. The next morning, I felt a strong urge to call any of my acquaintances who had done their mandatory service to ask if it was, but I also didn't want to be considered eccentric, as I felt I was being. To this day, I have not breathed a word of that night to anyone.

~

Alongside women unknown to me, I climbed down the well, helping them to hold on to their children. We thought it would be safe down there, but without warning a shower of bullets rained down on us from above. The women clasped the children against their bodies, shielding them as best they could. From the bottom of what we'd thought was a dry well, a grassy liquid, viscous like melted rubber, oozed out and quickly rose around us. Engulfing our blood and our screams.

~

I was walking along a deserted road with some companions whose faces I cannot recall. We came across a black passenger car parked on

the shoulder, and someone said, He's in there.
No name was mentioned, but we understood
immediately that the one who had ordered the
massacre that spring was in the car. As we stood
watching, the car pulled away and turned on to
the premises of a large stone building. Someone
said, We should follow. We headed towards the
building. There were several of us when we set
out, but by the time we stepped inside the empty
building, only two of us, including myself,
remained. Someone stood quietly by my side. I
sensed that the person was a man, and that he
seemed to be following me reluctantly. We were
only two – what could two people possibly do?
Light leaked from a room at the end of the dim
hall. When we stepped inside, the mass murderer
was standing with his back to a wall. He held a
lighted match in one hand. That's when I realized that my companion and I were each holding
a match as well. We could speak for as long as the
matches burned. No one had told us, but we
knew that was the rule. The murderer's match
was almost burned out, the flame down to his
thumb. Our matches remained but were burning
fast. Murderer, I thought I should say. I opened
my mouth.

Murderer.

My voice refused to come out.

Murderer.

Louder, I had to speak louder.

What are you going to do about all the people you've killed? I said, using every last ounce of energy I had.

Then I wondered if we were supposed to kill him now, if this would be the last chance any of us had. But how? How could we possibly? I glanced to my side and saw the orange flame of my companion's frail matchstick — my companion of faint face and breath — wane. In that light I sensed with vivid clarity how young the keeper of that match was. He was only a gangling boy.

～

I finished the manuscript and visited my publisher in January of the following year. I wanted to ask that they publish the book as quickly as possible. For I'd thought, foolishly, that once it was out, the nightmares would cease. My editor told me it would be better in terms of promotion to push the launch to May.

Wouldn't it be best to time the release so that

one more person is likely to pick it up? they asked.

I was persuaded by those words. While I waited, I rewrote another chapter of the book. Then it was the editor's turn to rush me, until I at last handed in the final manuscript in April. The book came out almost to the day in mid May. The nightmares, unsurprisingly, continued regardless. In retrospect it baffles me. Having decided to write about mass killings and torture, how could I have so naively – brazenly – hoped to soon shirk off the agony of it, to so easily be bereft of its traces?

⌒

Then there is the night I awoke from that black forest and covered my eyes with the palm of my cold hand.

Sometimes, with some dreams, you awake and sense that the dream is ongoing elsewhere. This dream is like that. As I eat my meals, drink my tea, ride the bus, walk hand in hand with my child, pack our bags ahead of a trip, or walk up the countless stairs out of a subway station, to one side of me it is perpetually snowing, over a

34

plain I have never visited. Over black trees chopped down to torsos, dazzling hexagonal crystals form, then crumble. Startled, my feet underwater, I look back. And there it is: the sea, rushing in.

Unable to let go of this scene, which rose up repeatedly before my mind's eye, that autumn, I had a thought. I could find a suitable place and plant some logs there, as they had appeared in my dream. Planting them in the thousands might not be feasible, but ninety-nine – a number that opens to infinity – could work; and then, together with a dozen or so people of shared purpose, we could clothe the trees in black meok. Ink them with the same devotion with which one might swaddle them in gowns woven out of deep night, so that their sleep may remain eternally unbroken. And once it was all done, we could wait. Not for the sea but for snow as white as cloth to drape down from the skies and blanket them all.

And the whole process could be documented in a short film, I suggested to a friend who had worked with photographs and on documentary features before. She readily agreed. We promised to see it through to fruition together but finding the right moment in both our schedules wasn't easy, and before long four years had drifted by.

~

Then there is the heat-drenched night I walk back through the baked-asphalt air to an empty house and a cold shower. Every evening the people in the flats above and below and to either side of me turn on their ACs, and I am forced to seal shut my own doors and windows against the infernal air spewing out of their fans. I take a seat at my desk in what may as well be a steam room, before the lingering coolness of the shower evaporates. The envelope containing my will sits on the desk, still unaddressed. I pick it up and tear it to pieces.

Start again.

A spell that is always right, always correct.

I start again. Within five minutes, sweat is running down my skin. I take another cold shower; I return to the desk. I rip up the terrible note I wrote a moment ago.

Start again.

Write a proper letter of farewell, a true leave-taking.

The previous summer, as my private life

began to crumble like a sugar cube dropped in water, back when the real partings that were to follow were only a premonition, I'd written a story titled 'Farewell', a story about a woman of snow who melts away under sleet. But that can't be my actual, final farewell.

Whenever the sweat stung my eyes too much to continue, I returned to the shower. Back at the desk, I'd shred what I'd written. When I eventually laid my clammy body on the floor, with yet another letter I had to begin anew remaining, the day was breaking blue. Like a blessing, I felt the temperature drop by a fraction. I thought I might be able to get some rest at last and was in fact half asleep, when the snow began drifting over the plain. A snow that seemed to have been falling for decades – no, centuries.

~

They're still safe.

That is what I told myself as I stared in defiance at the snowy field, refusing to turn away from the awareness that gripped me like a heavy, suspended blade.

The trees planted along the ridge to the top of the hill were safe, being outside the reach of the flood tide. The graves behind the copse were also safe, as the sea couldn't rise that high. The white bones of the hundreds buried there remained cool, clean and dry. The waves couldn't steal them away. Black trees stood their ground under falling snow, their bases neither wet nor rotting. A snow that had been falling for decades – no, centuries.

That's when I knew.

That I had to go, that I had to turn my back on the bones lower down, which were already lost to the billows. I had to head to the crest, before it was too late, parting the livid water that was now up to my knees. Waiting for no one, trusting no help would come, without hesitation, all the way up the brow. Up where I could see white snow crystals breaking over the woods.

There was no time.

It was the only way, that is

if I wanted to go on.

Go on living.

2

Threads

But I still had trouble sleeping.

I could barely eat.

My breath remained shallow.

I continued in the manner that those who left me had said they couldn't bear to witness.

The summer in which the world attempted to speak to me, relentlessly and at overwhelming volume, was over. I no longer had to sweat at every turn. I no longer had to lie on the floor, my body slack and listless. I no longer had to take endless cold showers.

A desolate boundary had formed between the world and me. I found a long-sleeved shirt and jeans, put them on and walked up the road, where the muggy air had lifted, to the juk shop. I still couldn't cook. Couldn't stomach more than one meal a day. Mostly I couldn't bear to remember what it was like to cook for or to share a meal with someone. But routine did return. I continued to meet no one and answer no calls, but I resumed checking my emails and phone messages with regularity. Every morning, at dawn, I sat at the desk and wrote, each time from scratch, a letter of farewell addressed to everyone.

By degrees night lengthened. With each day I noticed a cooling in the air. For the first time since I'd moved here, I went for a walk along the trail just behind the complex. It was early November and the tall maple trees were ablaze and glimmering in the sunlight. Beauty — but the wiring inside me that would sense beauty was dead or failing. One morning, the first frost of the season covered the half-frozen earth, and as the soles of my trainers touched the ground, I heard dry crunching. Brittle autumn leaves as big as young faces tumbled past me, and the limbs of the suddenly denuded plane trees, as their Korean name of buhzeum — flaking skin — suggests, resembled grey-white flesh stripped raw.

On that late December morning when I received Inseon's text message, I was on my way back from the trail. After a month of sub-zero temperatures, the hardwood trees had dropped all their leaves.

Kyungha-ya.

That was the entirety of her message: my name.

I met Inseon the year I graduated. I was hired by a magazine where the editors mostly took their own photographs, as the publisher didn't have photographers on payroll, but for important interviews and travel articles we'd pair up with freelancers we'd booked ourselves. Going on the road meant as many as three nights and four days spent in company, and, on the advice of my seniors, who said it was best for women to team up with women and men with men, I called round several photo production houses until I was introduced to Inseon, who happened to be the same age as me. For the next three years we went on monthly assignments together until I left the magazine, and as we'd been friends for well over two decades, by now I knew most of her habits. When she started a conversation by calling my name, I knew she wasn't simply checking in but had something specific and urgent she wanted to discuss.

Hi. Is everything all right?

I removed my woollen glove to send a reply, then waited. Seeing there was no answer, I was pulling the glove back on when another text arrived.

Can you come right away?

Inseon didn't live in Seoul. She was an only child, born when her mother was past forty, and thus encountered her mother's growing frailty earlier than most. Eight years ago, she returned to a mountain village in Jeju to care for her mother, whom she lost four years later; she'd remained in that house on her own ever since. Prior to that, Inseon and I used to drop by each other's place all the time to cook and eat together and to catch up, but what with the physical distance and each of us having to deal with life's curveballs, our visits grew less frequent and further apart. Eventually the interval grew to an entire year, then two. My most recent trip to Jeju was in autumn of the previous year. During the four days I stayed with her, in the unassuming stone house with its exposed wooden beams, a house that had been renovated only to the extent of having a toilet fitted indoors, she introduced me to a pair of small white budgies she'd brought home two years ago from one of the markets that opened every five days. One of the pair could even say a simple word or two. Then she led me across the yard to her carpentry workshop, where she said she spent the better part of her day. She showed me the chairs she'd made from tree stumps, planed but without any joinery. These sold fairly well for some reason and helped her make ends meet. Sit down, feel how comfortable it is, she urged. Later she threw some wild mulberries and raspberries in a kettle and made me a sour and rather bland tea over the wood stove. She'd picked the berries that summer in the woods above her place. While I drank the tea, grumbling about its taste, Inseon in her jeans and work shoes tied her hair firmly back, stuck a mechanical pencil behind her ear like some master artisan featured in a TV documentary, and got to work measuring and drawing lines on a board with a set square.

She couldn't mean come to her Jeju house. *Where are you?* I asked in my next text, just as Inseon's message arrived. It was the name of a hospital in Seoul, though one I wasn't familiar with. Then came the same question as before.

Can you come right away?

Then another message.

Bring ID.

I wondered if I should stop by my place first. I had on a long puffer coat that was two sizes too big, but at least it was clean. The wallet in my pocket contained a credit card I could use to withdraw cash, along with my ID card. I was halfway to the next subway station and the taxi rank there when I saw a free cab approach and waved it down.

⌒

The first thing I saw was the black lettering on the grimy banner boasting *Nation's Best*. I paid the fare and walked towards the hospital entrance, wondering why, if it really was the nation's best in surgical wound closures, I had never heard of the place before. I passed through the revolving door into a dimly lit lobby with worn finishing. On one wall there were some photographs of a hand and a foot, each missing a finger and a toe. I wanted to look away but forced myself to cast my eyes over them. Knowing my memory might distort the images into something more fearsome, I thought I may as well look. But I was wrong;

these photographs grew more painful the closer I observed them. My eyes reluctantly moved on to the next set of photos: the same hand and foot, now with sutured-on finger and toe. There was a marked difference in skin tone and texture on either side of the suture lines.

I realized Inseon must have had a similar accident in her workshop, that that must be why she was here.

There are people who actively change the course of their own life. They make daring choices that others seldom dream of, then do their utmost to be accountable for their actions and the consequences of those actions. So that in time, no matter what life path they strike out on, people around them cease to be surprised. After studying photography in college, Inseon developed an interest in documentary film-making in her late twenties and spent a decade steadily pursuing this badly paid profession. She of course took on any directing work that came her way to make ends meet, but as whatever money she made was rerouted back into her own films, she was always broke. She ate little, spent little and worked a lot. She packed a simple lunch wherever she went, wore no make-up and cut her own hair using a pair of thinning scissors. She sewed cardigans into the linings of her one cotton parka and her one coat to make them warmer. Amazingly these habits came across as natural, unaffected, even stylish.

Of the short films she made every couple of years, the first to receive favourable reviews was a series of interviews she'd done in the dense forests of Việt Nam. The women she'd interviewed spoke about the sexual assault perpetrated by Korean military personnel during the war. On the strength of that film, in which nature itself seemed the main subject, so arresting were the images of sunlight and thick tropical foliage, Inseon received a grant from a private cultural foundation to produce her next documentary. The resulting film had what was, for her, a relatively big budget, and focused on the daily life of an elderly woman who had been active in the armed groups in Manchuria fighting for Korean independence into the 1940s and who now had dementia. I liked this work: the quiet shots of the woman's empty eyes and her silence as she leaned on her daughter or used a cane to move about indoors, intercut with shots of the interminable winter forests on the plains of Manchuria. After this, everyone expected Inseon's next project to focus once again on testimonies of women whose lives had intersected with history, but, surprisingly, she turned the camera on herself. Shadows, knees, hands: a woman visible only as a faint figure sat in darkness, slowly piecing her words together. Unless you knew her well enough to recognize her voice, you couldn't tell that the interviewee was Inseon. Apart from brief cutaway shots showing black-and-white footage of Jeju in 1948, there was no clear narrative; the pauses between words were drawn out and long; and throughout its running time, smudges of light over a limewashed wall in shadow repeatedly faded and reappeared. The film left people perplexed and disappointed, especially those who had hoped for a reiteration of the straightforwardly moving accounts of her previous work. Irrespective of the response, Inseon had planned to pull the three shorts together to make her first feature-length documentary. Then for some unknown reason she shelved this triptych, as she called it, and instead applied and was admitted to carpentry school, the fees for which were covered by public funding.

I knew that Inseon was a regular at a

carpentry workshop near her home, that during periods when she wasn't working she would hole up there for days at a time to cut timber and measure and join panels to make her own furniture. I marvelled at it. Still, I couldn't quite believe that she'd quit film-making to become a carpenter. Nor was I entirely convinced when she told me of her decision to move down to Jeju permanently to care for her mother, before she'd even completed her one-year carpentry course. I assumed she'd spend some time reconnecting to her birthplace and soon return to resume her film work. But not long after she arrived in Jeju, Inseon set about converting the shed, once used to store harvested mandarins, into a workshop, and started making furniture. And when her mother's awareness slipped so much she couldn't be left alone, Inseon installed a small workbench in the central room of the main house and, with a hand plane and chisel, cut and shaped and oiled small wooden items, from chopping boards and trays to spoons and ladles. It wasn't until after her mother had passed away that she dusted and reorganized the workshop and went back to making larger items of furniture.

Inseon was slender but tall at five foot seven,

and I'd seen her handle and transport filming equipment since our twenties. I didn't consider her too frail for the job, even if I was surprised at her choice. I did worry about her frequent injuries, however. Not long after losing her mother, she'd got her jeans caught in an electric grinder and wound up with a thirty-centimetre scar from knee to thigh – I tried and tried to pull it out, but it was no good; the grinder kept roaring and turning and gosh, it was monstrous, she'd told me later, laughing – and two years ago, she'd broken her left index finger and ruptured a tendon while trying to stop a pile of logs she'd been loading from falling; she'd needed half a year of rehab and treatment.

But this time it must be worse. She must have severed something.

I had to ask for Inseon's room number, but a young couple were at the information desk, holding on to a child of about four or five with a bandaged hand. The adults looked both shocked and on the verge of tears. I couldn't approach the desk now; I stopped awkwardly in the middle of the lobby, then turned to look past the revolving door. It wasn't yet noon, but the light outside was murky. Under lowering skies that threatened snow, the concrete buildings across the road huddled their hard bodies in the cold damp air.

I should have some cash on me, I thought. Walking to an ATM at the end of the lobby, I wondered why my ID was needed. Perhaps they had proceeded with emergency surgery without a surrogate's consent and now required someone to guarantee payment. Given that Inseon had neither parents, nor siblings, nor a spouse.

～

Inseon-ah.

When I called her name, she was lying at the furthest end of the six-bed room, her eyes anxiously trained past the glass door I'd just entered. It wasn't me she was waiting for. Perhaps she was in urgent need of a nurse or a doctor? But then, as if suddenly coming to, Inseon recognized me. Her large eyes opened even wider and brightened, before growing as thin as two crescent moons nestled in a bed of fine lines.

You came.

I saw her mouth the words.

What happened? I asked, approaching her bed.

Above the loose-fitting patient garb, her thin

clavicle looked even more prominent. Her face
was about the only part of her that looked less
gaunt than when I'd seen her last, though perhaps this was due to swelling.

Sliced my fingers off, with the electric saw,
Inseon said in a whisper as if to minimize engaging
her vocal cords, which suggested she'd hurt her
throat rather than her fingers.

What? When? I asked.

Two mornings ago.

She slowly slid her hand towards me and
added, Want to see it?

Her hand wasn't entirely bandaged up as I'd
expected. The tips of her first and middle fingers,
both of which had been severed and reattached,
remained exposed. Bloodstains, a mixture of fresh
red and oxidized black, covered the sutures.

My eyelids must have blinked and fluttered.

Quite a sight, isn't it? Inseon said.

I looked at her, not knowing how to respond.

Well, I thought so, she said with a faint smile.
I noticed her pallor and wondered if she'd lost
too much blood. As for her whispering, I figured
again that the voicing alone must be causing
her pain.

I thought it was only a deep cut at first, she said.

Leaning down to hear her words, I caught a faint whiff of blood.

But soon the pain became excruciating, she continued. It was difficult, but I managed to peel the torn work glove off, and that's when I saw the fingertips.

I had to watch her mouth to hear her. Her bloodless lips had a purple hue.

Then the blood was gushing everywhere, she said. I remember thinking I had to staunch it, but beyond that it's a complete blank.

I saw her face flicker with self-reproach.

It doesn't matter how cold your hands get, she said, you never wear cotton work gloves when you're using power tools. It was entirely my mistake.

Hearing someone open the room's glass door, Inseon turned her head. From the sudden relief on her face, I knew it must be whomever she'd been waiting for earlier. A woman with short hair and a brown apron who looked to be in her early sixties approached us.

This is my friend, Inseon said to the woman. Then, to me: She's been taking care of me. In alternate shifts, during the day.

The kindly-looking carer smiled and said

hello. She pumped some hand sanitizer into her palms – I could smell the alcohol from where I stood – and rubbed it meticulously into both hands, then brought over an aluminium box from the bedside table and placed it on her lap.

The part that was basically a miracle, Inseon resumed, was that an elderly woman I'm friendly with and who lives down the way from me had an appointment at the big university hospital that day, and so her son had come to drive her into downtown Jeju.

As Inseon spoke, the aluminium box opened with a click. Two syringes of differing sizes, a bottle of alcohol disinfectant, a plastic case of sterile cotton and a pair of tweezers were laid in a neat row inside.

The son delivers parcels and has a truck, Inseon was saying, and as the woman meant to drop off a box of mandarins for me, they stopped by my house. When I didn't come to the door, though the light was on in my workshop, they stepped inside to check if everything was okay and found me lying there, unconscious. There was a lot of blood so they first tried to stem the bleeding, then carried me to the back of the truck and rushed to the hospital. She was clutching the glove that held my amputated fingertips on the drive over. Then, since there's no hand surgeon on the island, they got me on the earliest flight to Seoul—

Inseon's whisper was interrupted. The carer had jabbed a needle into the still-bloody suture of Inseon's index finger. Inseon's hand and lips trembled simultaneously. I saw the carer proceed to disinfect a second needle with an alcohol-soaked cotton ball and once again, deftly and without hesitation, she pricked Inseon's middle finger, in order to wound it. Inseon didn't open her mouth again until after the woman had disinfected and replaced both needles in the aluminium container.

They say the surgery went well, she said.

Though she was still whispering, voiced sounds did creep in between her words now and then, perhaps from the strain of trying to stifle the pain.

The important thing now is to make sure the bleeding doesn't stop, she said.

Inseon was mustering all her strength to whisper, and I found the news anchor's voice booming from the mounted TV by the room's entrance annoyingly tiresome.

We have to make sure scabs don't form on the wound, Inseon went on. They said we have to let the blood flow, that I have to feel the pain. Otherwise the nerves below the cut will die.

And what happens if they die? I asked numbly.

Inseon brightened suddenly and I almost found myself smiling back at her beaming, child-like face.

They'll rot, of course. The reattached tips.

She widened her eyes as if to add, Obviously, but I could only stare back at her.

So we do this every three minutes, to prevent that from happening, Inseon said. Round the clock, with the carers taking shifts.

Every three minutes? I seemed to have lost the ability to say anything that wasn't an echo of her words. But what about sleep?

I just lie here in bed, and the night carer sits and dozes by my side when she's not poking me with the needles.

And you have to do this for how long?

Another three weeks.

I stared at Inseon's fingers, freshly bloodied and swollen and looking even more livid than before. I raised my head, wanting to look away, only to meet Inseon's eyes.

Horrible, aren't they?

No, I said.

They look horrible to me, she said.

No, really, I said, lying a second time.

Honestly, I'd rather give up, Kyungha.

Inseon wasn't lying.

Of course the doctors assume I'll stick with it. The right index finger is pretty essential after all.

Inseon's eyes were bright beneath her darkened lids. If only I'd let go of them right at the start, she said, then we'd have simply stitched up the stubs and been done with it back in Jeju.

I shook my head.

You work with cameras, I said. You need that finger to work the shutter, don't you?

Yes, you're right, she said. And even if I were to give up now, the doctors don't recommend it because a lot of people go on to live with the pain.

I understood then that Inseon had seriously considered amputation as an option. Perhaps every three minutes, as she endured the needles. Hence the discussion with her doctors. Asking if she couldn't simply let them go. And the doctors would have told her about phantom pain. That while the pain of keeping her fingers intact may feel greater now, if she gave up on reattaching them, she would have to live in agony for which there would be no remedy or relief.

Three weeks is far too long, I muttered, not knowing if these words offered comfort. Not to mention the price of aftercare.

Right, because this isn't covered by insurance, Inseon replied. I heard that people who have families don't hire carers for that reason. Of course, all this is a lot tougher to stomach the closer you are to the patient, but options are limited if you're on a tight budget.

I admit I felt relieved at that moment. That I wasn't her family, that the task of sticking needles into her at three-minute intervals wouldn't fall to me. It was only later that I wondered how Inseon would cover the hospital bill. As far as I knew, during the four years she was caring for her mother, Inseon had chipped away at the large sum she'd brought with her when she'd moved to Jeju, the money she'd used as her jeonse rent deposit in Seoul. Though she managed to meet her own modest cost of living through the sale of her handcrafted furniture and wooden dinnerware, I doubted she had any savings put away for emergencies such as this. *I only have myself to think about now, so I'm not worried*, had been

Inseon's reply when I'd once asked how she was doing for money. *I have an overdraft account, but I only draw from it occasionally. I'm usually never in the red, and at times I'm far, far from it . . . On the whole, things roll along pretty smoothly.*

~

Wait, is that snow?

I started at Inseon's words and glanced behind me.

Outside the large window that faced out on to a road, a sparse snow was falling. I watched the white thread-like flakes draw empty paths through the air. Looking about, I saw that patients and guardians alike were silently gazing out at the snowfall, their blank faces suggesting a familiarity with pain and endurance.

I studied Inseon's profile as she looked out of the window. There are people who, though not notably handsome, give the impression of beauty; she was one of them. It was the sharp gleam in her eyes, partly; but, more than that, I was convinced it was due to her personality and the care she took with words, as well as her general demeanour, which suggested she was unlikely to struggle with chaos or lethargy. A brief conversation with her, and the realm of confusion, ambiguity and uncertainty seemed, on the whole, to recede. Her words and gestures revealed a quiet strength, which made you believe that all our acts had purpose; that even when it led to failure, every attempt we made was meaningful. She remained poised even now, despite her bloodied hand, her loose hospital gown and the I V line dangling from her forearm. She didn't appear frail or crushed in the least.

Looks like a big storm, doesn't it? she said.

I nodded in reply. It really did. The light had dimmed considerably.

It feels strange to be watching the snow with you, she said, turning to look at me.

I had been thinking the same thing. Snow had an unreality to it. Was this because of its pace or its beauty? There was an accompanying clarity to snow as well, especially slow, drifting snow. What was and wasn't important were made distinct. Certain facts became chillingly apparent. Pain, for one. That I had held on for months out of a paradoxical determination to finish my will. That this respite from my own hell to visit a friend in hospital felt unnerving in its peculiarity and its striking lucidity.

But by 'strange', I knew that Inseon meant something different.

⌣

Four years ago, in late autumn, Inseon chose not to inform most of her acquaintances in Seoul about her mother's passing, though she did let me know. Late in the night, when the neighbours had come and gone and the few film people I'd met once or twice before had left to catch their flights, the hospital funeral hall had grown quiet. Aren't you tired? Inseon asked, but I shook my head no. I felt I should keep the conversation going for her sake, but I didn't know what to say to a friend whose day-to-day I hadn't kept up with in so long. As her mother grew increasingly frail, Inseon had refused my visits. My calls to her often went unanswered and she didn't ring back right away. When I texted to ask how she was doing, she wouldn't reply for days. Reading her brief, calm messages, which gave no indication as to how she was feeling, only emphasized our distance: *Everything's as usual with me. I hope you're well.* With such a gulf between us, after all this time, could I even ask her what she planned to do next?

I think these complicated feelings were what prompted me to tell her about my dream that night, when she asked me how I'd been. I dreamed it back in the summer but it stayed with me all these months and now it's almost winter, I confided to her over a plate of peeled mandarins and jeolpyeon that neither of us had touched. I told her how I'd be trudging over a seemingly interminable crossing at an eight-lane road to get to the hospital for my recurrent abdominal spasms, or crouching in a corner of a noisy café with my eyes on the entrance, waiting for someone to show up, or staring up at the darkness of the ceiling, head trembling, after startling awake from yet another nightmare, and the scene would appear before me: the white snow over the plain, the seawater pushing in through the black trees.

Which is why I wanted to ask you — what if we did something about it together? I asked Inseon. What if you and I were to plant logs in a field, dress them in black ink and film them under falling snow?

Well, we'd have to get started before autumn

ends, Inseon answered after listening to all I had to say. She was dressed in the black hanbok of mourning, her chin-length hair tied back with a white rubber band and her face earnest and composed. She said to plant ninety-nine logs in a field, we had to be sure the ground wasn't frozen. She suggested we gather people to help with the planting by mid November at the latest, and said we could use the abandoned tract of land she'd inherited from her father, which no one used.

Does the ground freeze here too? I asked.

Of course, the uplands are frozen throughout the winter, she said.

Will it snow heavily enough to film? I'd prefer it if we got larger flakes on camera.

I had a few questions as I'd never considered Jeju as a possible site for the project. Jeju was an island of trees from temperate and subtropical climates – I doubted it saw much snowfall. I'd always assumed the best region for the project would be somewhere colder than Seoul, like the border region in the north-eastern province of Gangwon-do.

Oh, snow is the one thing you don't have to worry about, Inseon said, her eyes crinkling. It was the first time she'd smiled that day. She told me that their village was damp and saw a lot of rain and fog and snow, and in spring the fog got so thick the women, deprived of sunlight, would complain of chronic depression. Aside from the frequent downpours in summer, rain fell two or three times a week, even in spring and autumn, and the region often saw heavy snowfall well into March.

The hardest part will be the woodwork that has to be done before, she said. And finding enough hands to do the actual planting, all of that has to be meticulously planned. But getting footage of falling snow is easy. I can get hours of film for you in my spare time.

We were set to start right away, that very winter, but some personal matters came up as soon as I returned to Seoul and the work had to be postponed. Then other things thwarted us. Some years it was Inseon, other years it was me, but one or the other of us wouldn't be in the right place or in good health. Then the first snow would fall and I'd think to myself, Not this year either then. One of us would pick up the phone first and say, It's snowing here – is it snowing there? And the other one would answer, It should do tomorrow. Will we get around to it next year?

one would ask, and the other one would say, Yes, we really should. Then we'd burst out laughing. Sometimes I wondered if this constant deferral was itself becoming a key aspect of the project.

~

Click. The aluminium case was reopened. I watched nervously as the carer pumped a generous amount of sanitizer into her hands and rubbed it between her fingers. Inseon herself seemed oblivious to the sound and looked quietly up at me as if she couldn't guess where my eyes were trained.

The monotony is what worries me, she said. They tell me I have to stay bed-bound, like this, for as long as I'm here. A grumbling smile was on Inseon's lips. I can't walk, and I can't do anything that puts even the slightest pressure on my arm.

The carer disinfected two needles. Then she sanitized her hands again, I supposed to make sure they hadn't carried over any germs from the needles.

The nerves they've bundled up could easily loosen again, Inseon went on. Then they'd snap up past my elbow and the doctors would have to put me under general anaesthesia and open my arm up to the shoulder to find them again. Earlier this year, they had a patient who didn't wake up afterwards and had to be transported to a big hospital. Not to mention someone who died from sepsis a few years back.

Inseon stopped speaking. I held my breath too and watched as the carer slid the needle into Inseon's open wound with the same deft movement as before, then immediately regretted not turning my head away. Hadn't I learned already, down in the lobby, that looking squarely at the injury made it all the more excruciating?

As the carer moved on to Inseon's middle finger, I shifted my eyes to the mobile phone by Inseon's pillow. I could guess the cautious manipulation of the waist, shoulders and left hand that must have been involved for Inseon to compose and send a text message without the use of her dominant hand. *Can you come right away?* All her effort to combine vowels with consonants, to insert spaces and question marks to ask this of me, twice. But why had it been me?

I knew she didn't have a lot of friends and only stayed in touch with a few people who shared her temperament. But it hadn't occurred to me that I might be the first person she'd think of in a situation like this. This past summer, when I considered to whom my last wishes might be addressed, Inseon hadn't crossed my mind. Her being relatively far away likely had a lot to do with this. And I'd had no wish to burden Inseon again after the four years she'd spent caring for her ailing mother and then sitting vigil with her in her final moments. But even if it was true that Inseon had distanced herself from me during that period and I'd had my own trials, couldn't I have made more of an effort? After all, the island was only an hour's flight away, if that. Surely I could have thought of something, something other than letting her drift out of reach?

I think these swirling thoughts were what prompted me to say, You'll be all right. I'd intended to reassure her, but the words emerged as a question. I saw her lips quiver with the renewed pain in her fingers. She seemed to momentarily dissociate. Her eyes were on me, though I was sure I'd never seen them look so empty in all the time I'd known her.

Was rousing such agonizing pain the only

way to keep the threads of nerves intact? I couldn't believe it. Could twenty-first-century medicine offer no alternative? Could it be that Inseon had been rushed to a small hospital unable to offer better care on the basis of its proximity to the airport?

The light returned to Inseon's eyes. I'd assumed she hadn't heard my thoughtless question, but now she whispered, as if the question merited a response, I guess I'll have to carry on. For now.

This was a favourite saying of hers. Back when we used to travel for work, whenever we had to deal with a problematic interviewee or sort out issues with the location we'd booked and I would be rushing about all flustered, Inseon, despite being the same age as me, always remained calm and would say in an easy-going voice, *Well, I'll carry on in any case.* When I returned after having either resolved or partly dealt with the issue or having failed to find a solution, Inseon would be waiting with her equipment set up, and somehow would have won everyone at the location over to her side. With her camcorder in place ahead of the interviews or in her hands if we were taking stills, she would flash a smile at me and say, Start whenever you want. That smile would buoy my heart, and seeing my face brighten, Inseon's eyes in turn would shine.

I'll carry on in any case.

How those words set me at ease. No matter how demanding our interviewee turned out to be, no matter what curveballs we were thrown and how ruffled I might be, the simple act of watching Inseon's serene face as she peered at the viewfinder would always instil a sense of calm in me.

It occurred to me that she had said those exact words in our last phone conversation.

Back in August, after encountering the plain of black trees again as I wandered between dream and reality in the early hours, I'd finally opened my eyes and made my escape. Forcing my sweaty body up off the floor, I walked to the enclosed balcony. I felt a brief, cool breeze as I opened the windows, but in a matter of minutes the humid air was rushing in and heating up the room.

The cicadas were screeching. And had been all night, I soon recalled. Not long after, the outdoor AC units of my neighbours on either side and below whirred back into motion. I closed the windows and walked over to the bathroom to wash away the mugginess that enveloped me like a layer of salt. There was no running away or hiding from the heat. I lay down on the floor of the sitting room with the phone by my head, and waited for seven o'clock. That was about the only time I could catch Inseon over the phone, as she was in her workshop from early morning until six in the evening each day, and kept her mobile on silent while she worked.

Yes, Kyungha, Inseon answered in her usual warm and easy manner. How have you been?

We briefly exchanged pleasantries and then I told her I thought it best not to go ahead with the black-trees project. I said I had misunderstood the dream from the beginning. I told her I was sorry. And that we would talk about it at length later.

I see, Inseon answered when I had said my piece. But the thing is, she said, I've already started. I started right after your last visit actually.

The previous autumn in Jeju, Inseon had brought up the project without prompting from me. I think I'm ready to start now, she'd said, and I'd agreed that we should move ahead with it. Then I'd gently asked her if she'd worked on any films since moving to Jeju. And whether she planned to get back to it. Inseon was silent for a while. *Yes*, she'd finally said, *maybe I could*.

Now she said, I collected the logs all winter, Kyungha.

As though she'd anticipated my call and had prepared a script to catch me up, Inseon began quietly and methodically explaining the steps.

I gathered plenty more logs than the ninety-nine we needed and started airing them out in spring. They're humid again now that it's summer, but by October they'll have dried just the right amount. I'll work hard until November so we can plant them before the ground freezes. Then we can film them from December right through March, whenever it snows.

That she may have started prepping for the project had occurred to me, hence my phone call, but I was stunned nonetheless. Some part of me had thought the project would never come to fruition, for whatever reason, as had been the case for four years.

Well, couldn't you use those logs to make something else? I asked.

Inseon laughed. No, she said, they can't be used for anything else.

I was well aware of Inseon's habit of revealing her feelings by subtly tempering her laughter. Yes, she laughed out of delight and amusement, with warmth and a sense of mischief too, but she also tended to laugh before turning someone down or when she was about to voice a different opinion and did not wish to argue.

I'm sorry, Inseon, I apologized again. But I think it's best that we don't. I'm serious.

The laughter now completely gone from her voice, Inseon asked, Maybe you'll have a change of heart?

No, that won't happen, I said. I felt the need to make this clear. It's my fault, I said. I misjudged all of it.

The silence on the other end felt a lot longer than the few seconds it actually lasted.

Finally she said, Well, I'll carry on in any case.

There's no reason to, Inseon, I said, trying to dissuade her.

It's all right, she said as though in a generous

response to an apology. Her voice was full of patience, as if she were the one appeasing me. I'm fine, Kyungha. You don't have to worry.

⌣

Click. The unbearable sound of the aluminium box being reopened. Another three minutes had passed. The carer's eyes met mine and she said, as if to explain herself, Your friend is amazingly strong. She's bearing all this so well.

Inseon indicated neither agreement nor disagreement, but simply extended her right arm, slowly. The blood-soaked bandage wound about her hand looked too saturated. Had a nurse come by in the morning to apply a new dressing and rebandage the hand? Were they doing so regularly enough, what with the constant bleeding?

The doctors and nurses all say so, you know, the carer continued. That she's being so incredibly brave.

While the needles plunged into her wounds, Inseon pursed her lips and looked towards the window. Outside, minuscule ice crystals were drawing thin lines in the air as they descended.

The strangest thing, snow, Inseon said in a whisper I could barely hear. How does something like that fall from the sky?

~

She went on whispering, as though she didn't need me to answer her, as though she were speaking to someone else.

I came to in the back of the delivery truck
  and felt a terrifying pain pulsating from my fingers.
  A pain I hadn't ever imagined
  and that I can't now put into words.
  I hadn't the faintest idea how much time had passed,
  or who was taking me or where we were headed.
  All I could do was guess, from the endless stream of trees visible out of the corner of my eye, that the truck was driving over Hallasan.
  Parcel boxes, thick rubber cords, grimy blankets, a cart with rusty wheels, and there I was too, writhing like a half-dead insect.
  I thought I'd black out from the pain,
  I thought I'd rather black out than go on feeling

it, but instead, I've no idea why, I remembered your book.

The people in your book — no, the people who were actually there at the time.

No, not just the people who were there, but everyone who's ever suffered similar fates regardless of place.

Hit with bullets,
hit with cudgels,
lives severed by blades.
How agonizing it must have been
when it hurts this much to have the tips of one's fingers sliced off.
Everyone who's ever met such violent death, everyone who's ever been pierced or stabbed
to the point their breath itself was excised.

~

That's when I knew that Inseon had been thinking of me all this time. Or, more precisely, about the project we'd promised to collaborate on. Or, even more precisely, about the black trees from my dream four years ago. And the book, which was the source of that dream.

The next moment an even more terrifying

intuition occurred and I stopped breathing. This summer, Inseon had told me she'd got the timber together. That she was drying well over a hundred uncut logs already. That she would start sawing and chopping and carving come autumn to make life-sized stooped and leaning figures to resemble a group of huddled people.

⌒

Was that what you were working on? I slowly managed, feeling that there was no escape. The project I said we shouldn't go ahead with? Is that how this happened?

I told you we shouldn't do it. I was so clear. Why did you have to be so headstrong? But this I couldn't say. I shouldn't have suggested it at all. I had no business telling you about a dream I barely understood. I shouldn't have roped you in.

That's not important, Kyungha, Inseon replied in what I felt sure was a roundabout affirmative, then rushed to say the next thing, as if to evade any apology or expressions of self-reproach and regret from me. She wasn't whispering any more. Her voice was suddenly clear, as though she no longer felt pain.

The reason I asked you to come today has nothing to do with any of that, she said. I have a favour to ask of you.

Unable to look away from her eyes, which were suddenly alive and gleaming, I waited for her to continue.

3

Heavy Snow

At first, I mistake them for birds. Tens of thousands of white-feathered birds flying right along
the horizon.

In fact, they are snow clouds scattered by
strong gusts of wind over the offing. Snowflakes
glisten in the sunlight shining between the clouds.
The doubling effect from the light reflecting off
the surface of the ocean has created an illusion:
white birds sweeping over the sea in a long, shimmering band.

This is the first time I've witnessed such a storm.
Once, ten winters ago, I saw snow heaped up to
my knees on the streets of Seoul, but the snowfall
itself hadn't been so dense as to fill the sky like
this. Inland cities didn't get these kinds of winds.
Now, seat belt on, sitting at the front of a bus
making its way down a coastal road as the storm

bears down, I look out at the palm trees swaying in the gale. I know the wet surface of the roads must be near freezing, but it feels unreal to watch this much snow simply vanish, not a trace of it sticking to the ground. At times the wind comes to a sudden stop due to atmospheric forces I can't fathom, and then enormous snowflakes descend from the sky so slowly that I imagine, if I were not on a moving bus, I would be able to see each crystal, each perfect hexagon, with my naked eye. But when the wind picks up again, the snowflakes swirl wildly as if inside a giant popcorn machine. As if snow did not fall from the sky but instead sprang up infinitely from the earth to be sucked into the void.

I start to feel uneasy. Wondering if I made the right choice in getting on the bus.

The plane I'd been on two hours earlier made an extremely shaky landing at Jeju Airport. It must have been the 'wind shear' I had only ever heard about on the news. As our plane slowed to a stop on its glide down the runway, the young woman seated across the aisle from me tapped on her phone and murmured, Oh no, every flight after our next one is cancelled. The young man with her, who appeared to be her partner, remarked,

Lucky us. The woman laughed. You call this lucky? Are you seeing this weather?

When I made it out of the airport, the snow was coming down so strong I couldn't fully open my eyes. After yielding four taxis to the people behind me in the queue, I crossed the street again and headed back towards the airport. I approached a porter in a neon vest who had been loading suitcases on to a limousine bus and asked if he knew why I'd been denied service. When he heard where I was headed, the older man advised me to take the bus. Both yellow and amber warnings for snow and high wind had been issued for the island, and he didn't think any cabs would be willing to go all the way out to the village in the uplands where Inseon lived. He said all the buses, no matter the route, would put on their tyre chains and continue to run, but if it snowed through the night they too would suspend operations, and there was a good chance the uplands would be marooned starting from tomorrow morning. Which bus do I take? I asked. The man shook his head, brows furrowed from the snow gusting into his eyes and nose. Catch any one of the buses running from here and head to the bus terminal first, he said. From there, you can get to any place you'd like to go.

I took his advice, got on the first bus I saw and headed to the terminal. I was anxious. It would be dark by five o'clock, and it was already half past two. Inseon's house was isolated from the rest of the village. I would have to walk at least another half-hour from the bus stop to reach it. It didn't seem possible to find my way alone in this weather. Even Inseon had needed a torch to navigate the road up to her place at night, grumbling about the absence of street lamps. All the same, I couldn't just book a place to stay in downtown Jeju and wait until morning. Hadn't the man at the airport said the hill roads could be closed off tonight?

Not long after I arrived at the bus terminal, an express circle bus pulled in. This bus stopped at P——, the southern coastal town closest to Inseon's village. There were bus routes passing through or around Hallasan, but as those buses came few and far between and I would have had to wait more than an hour for the next one, I got on the express bus. Inseon had told me that whenever she had to visit the post office or the bank, she would drive her mini truck down to P——. I had sat in the passenger seat beside her as we rode through a dense camellia grove that appeared as the road began to slope downwards, the small flowering trees spread out endlessly on either side. She told me the bus that connected the town and her village came three times an hour. When she had nothing to carry and the weather was nice, she would catch that bus instead of taking the truck into town to walk along the shore. When I asked her where she liked to walk, her eyes indicated the sand beach over which the sea, a breathtaking blue, was rolling in and cresting with foam.

Because I recalled these details vividly, I believed I was making the best possible choice at that moment: taking the first bus to P— before transferring to the local bus to make the rest of the trip to Inseon's village. But the island shoreline was essentially an elongated oval that ran east to west. I didn't know if it would have been quicker in the end to have waited at the terminal for another hour and caught the bus that travelled north to south through Hallasan. And I didn't know if, as the express bus took me around the island, the small local bus that would get me to Inseon's village would have stopped running on account of the snow.

The subtropical trees, weighed down with huge crimson blossoms, are swaying fiercely. The only reason not a dusting of snow has settled on the flowers in this strong storm is because of the overpowering wind. The movement of the palm trees, fronds swinging like so many long arms, seems even more violent. The glossy leaves, the flower stalks, the laden branches on every tree are flailing wildly, each like a separate entity trying to rid itself of the heavy snow.

Compared to this storm, the snowfall in Seoul had been peaceful. The snow I had seen not even four hours earlier as I left the hospital and climbed into a taxi had resembled countless white threads finely stitching the expanse between asphalt and ashen sky. Inseon, who was drawing fresh blood with the prick of a needle every three minutes, who was speaking in a whisper so as not to strain her vocal cords, who had looked at me with glistening eyes, whether because of the pain or some other emotion, I couldn't be sure – the taxi sped away from her, towards Gimpo Airport, as the wipers tirelessly cleared the snowflakes clinging like wet bits of string to the glass.

I have made my way here at Inseon's request. Because she said, I need you to go to my place in Jeju.

When? I asked.

Today. Before the sun sets.

What she was asking was close to impossible. Even if I took the quickest route from the hospital to the airport and managed to get on the next flight out to Jeju. I thought she was making an obscure joke, but she looked perfectly serious.

If you don't, she'll die.

Who will?

My bird.

I was about to ask what bird when I remembered the budgies I'd met when I visited her the previous autumn. One of the birds had greeted me hello and started chattering. I was surprised at how similar its voice was to Inseon's. I hadn't known budgies could imitate not only human pronunciation but vocal tones as well. Even more remarkable was that the bird had been able to carry on a quite plausible conversation by responding to Inseon's questions with a mix of quips like 'sure' and 'yeah', 'no' and 'dunno'. It's not fair to use the word 'parrot' to imply simple imitation, Inseon said. Not when a bird and I can converse like this. Sensing my uncertainty, she urged me, Go ahead — try talking to him. Tell him to come and sit on your hand. I hesitated, but her smile emboldened me to open the door of the birdcage and hold out my finger. Want to sit here? I asked. To my embarrassment, the bird immediately answered, No. Then, as if cancelling out what he had just said, he hopped on to my finger. I remembered feeling moved by his near weightlessness, the scratch of his tiny feet against my skin.

Ami died a few months ago, Inseon continued. Now only Ama is left.

If I remembered correctly, Ami was the bird that had spoken to me. The one with yellow streaks on his otherwise white head and tail, of a paler yellow than lemon. Inseon had told me her birds were expected to live for another ten years — what had brought on Ami's sudden death?

Please go and see if Ama is still alive, Inseon said. If she is, give her water.

Unlike Ami, Ama was completely white from crown to tail, which made her look more plain, and, though she didn't speak, she could perfectly echo the sound of Inseon's humming. Ama had flown up on to my shoulder at almost the same time that Ami had come to perch on my finger, and I could feel her body, as light as Ami's, and the same rough texture of her feet through the fabric of my sweater. When I'd turned to look at her, the little one tilted her head and, for a few seconds, met my gaze with her left eye, which appeared almost pensive.

All right, I said, nodding, weighing the seriousness of Inseon's request. I'll go home, pack, then get on the first flight out tomorrow morning at dawn—

That won't work.

I was a little surprised, as it was not like Inseon to interrupt.

That'll be too late, she said. It's already been a couple of days since the accident. I was rushed into surgery that night and incoherent until yesterday. I contacted you today as soon as the anaesthesia wore off.

Is there no one in Jeju you could ask?

No one, she said.

I found this hard to believe.

Not even in downtown Jeju or Seogwipo? What about the woman who found you?

I don't know her phone number.

Han Kang

I thought I heard a hint of unusual urgency in her tone.

I'd like you to go, Kyungha. Look after Ama in that house. Just until I'm released.

What are you saying? I wanted to ask, but she continued before I could cut in.

Luckily, I filled her water dish the other morning. And made sure she had a good amount of millet, dried fruit and pellets too, in case I was working until late in the evening. It might have been just enough to survive on for two days. But not three. If you can get to her today, there's a chance she might still make it. But by tomorrow she'll be dead. That's for sure.

I understand, I said in an attempt to soothe her, but I couldn't wrap my head around her insistence. I can't stay in your house by myself until you're released, though. I'll go down there and make sure the bird pulls through, then I'll bring her up here, in her cage. You'll feel better once you can see for yourself that she's all right.

No. Inseon held firm. Ama, she won't be able to handle such a sudden change in environment.

I was at a loss. In our twenty years of friendship, Inseon had never once asked me for such

72

an unreasonable favour. When she'd texted me to say I would need to bring some form of ID, I'd assumed the situation was urgent, that she needed me to sign a consent form for surgery or something similarly pressing. Which was why I'd jumped in a taxi straight away, without even stopping by my house. Was the pain and shock of this ordeal causing Inseon to act differently? Was she holding me responsible for what had happened while she was working on the project I'd suggested? Or was I really the only person she could ask? The only person who could drop everything at a moment's notice to spend close to a month in Jeju looking after a bird, someone who no longer had a job or family or meaning-ful daily routine to attend to? No matter the reason, one thing was certain. I couldn't turn her down.

◡

Each time the raging winds scatter dark clouds over the offing, sunlight falls on the horizon. Snowflakes resembling a flock of tens of thou-sands of birds appear like a mirage and sweep over the sea, vanishing with the light. I press my forehead against the cold windowpane by my seat. The front wipers squeak back and forth as, outside, an endless barrage of large snowflakes pummels the bus and disappears.

I sit up straight and dig inside my coat pocket. My hand brushes against a thin pack of gum. I had bought it in a rush at a convenience store in Gimpo Airport as my boarding time was drawing near. I'd popped a square of gum into my mouth as the plane was taking off, and now I push a second piece out through the blister-pack foil and start chewing. I can sense a migraine coming on like ice cracking in the distance. I have no idea what causes these headaches, which last ages and are accompanied by terrible abdominal spasms and a drop in blood pressure. Never knowing when one might begin, I've taken to carrying medicine most days, but since I more or less came straight here, I don't have any on me. However, once the prelude is over and the real symptoms start, any emergency prescription is useless. In my experience, gum is the only thing that helps in that critical moment right before a migraine begins in earnest. And once a migraine is under way, even the mildest juk does more harm than good as I can't keep anything down.

Where are you headed? the bus driver shouts in Jeju-mal. I don't have a bag with me and my oversized clothes don't look like those of a tourist. He must think I'm from here.

To P——, I say.

Where?

I speak up. Could you let me know when we get to P——?

Though we aren't far from each other, it seems the driver hasn't heard me clearly. The roar of the wind outside drowns me out. I assume he's asking for my destination because most of the stops we've passed by have been empty. I'm the only passenger on the bus, so if he sees from afar that no one is waiting at the upcoming stops, he can drive past without slowing down.

But at the very next stop someone is waiting to get on. A man in his thirties who looks to be a tourist is leaning into the road and waving his arms in the storm. As if he's exhausted himself from standing around in the raging winds, the man climbs aboard the bus and slumps into the seat behind the driver without paying the fare. Only after he manages to shrug off his heavy-looking backpack and set it down on the seat next to him does he reach inside his jacket pocket and pull out a wallet.

This bus goes to the airport, right? he asks, tapping his transportation card against the reader.

Ah, the driver shouts in reply. For the airport, you should catch the bus going the opposite way. And no planes are taking off now.

You're not going to the airport? The man's voice is edged with an almost despairing fatigue. The route is clearly posted on the front of the bus, isn't it? It says this bus goes to the airport.

It does, it does. But I'm saying this bus goes the long way, so you should catch the one already going in that direction.

I've waited all this time. As long as this bus gets there in the end, I'm taking it.

Could take us another two hours, though, says the driver, clicking his tongue. Well, if you want to go the long way round, I won't stop you, but like I said, the planes are all grounded for the rest of the day.

I'm aware of that. I'm going to wait at the airport until tomorrow morning, says the man.

Though he has been nothing but polite so far, he seems to be tamping down his growing irritation with the bus driver, who keeps slipping into over-familiar speech.

Wait at the airport until morning? But they cut the lights off and kick everyone out at eleven.

Are you saying I can't stay there overnight? The man seems surprised. What about the people who weren't able to catch their flights today?

What do you mean? They'll need to find places to stay, of course . . . You're really in a bind, huh? Caught out in this weather with no backup plan.

The driver side-eyes the man in his rear-view mirror, shaking his head at the sight of his baffled face, his open mouth.

The exchange ends there. Looking resigned, the man puts on his seat belt and takes out his phone. He's probably searching for accommodation in the downtown Jeju area or else reaching out to people he knows. I shift my gaze to the window facing inland, which the man's backpack half obscures. We are supposed to be headed towards a dormant volcano that stands at almost two thousand metres above sea level, but outside I see no such thing. A white mass of storm clouds and snow mist fill the air, rolling through the sky. The snow is falling in such a way that it doesn't accumulate much on the coast, but at a slightly higher altitude the situation will be different. Up in those hills and woods and pastures, there will be nothing so merciful as the sunlight that falls like a miracle when the clouds momentarily disperse, nor any of the glittering snowflakes that flurry over the surface of the sea like low-flying birds. Once we reach P—, we will have no choice but to enter into the heart of that white-out in all its stifling density.

Is Inseon used to this kind of snow? Would a blizzard like this have been surprising or out of the ordinary for her? This rolling grey mass of cloud, fog and snow. The fact that her childhood home exists as a precise location inside that huge storm, and that there is a bird – perhaps still breathing, perhaps not – waiting in that home.

That first year we started travelling together for work, because Inseon never brought up her hometown and spoke without a noticeable accent,

I assumed she had been born and raised in Seoul. Then one night I heard her talking to her mother on the payphone in the lobby of our lodgings and realized she was from the island. She spoke in a dialect that was hard for me to understand aside from a handful of nouns. Smiling, she asked a string of questions, made a few playful remarks, then laughed at some private joke before setting down the receiver.

What were you and your mum talking about that was so funny? I asked.

Nothing much. She was telling me about another basketball game she saw on TV, Inseon replied easily, her smile lingering. My mum is like any other grandmother, really, she went on. She was over forty when she had me and is well into her sixties now. She doesn't know the rules that well and watches mainly for the crowd. She gets lonely when there's no work since her place is so out of the way.

She sounded impish, like someone letting slip their best friend's little quirks.

She's still working at her age?

Of course. The women work even into their eighties. When it's time to harvest mandarins, they help out in each other's orchards.

Inseon smiled again, returning to the earlier topic.

She likes to watch football too. Even bigger crowds. She watches marches and protests on the news with the same interest. Like she's hoping to spot somebody she knows.

After that day, whenever there was a lull, whether on trains and buses, or in restaurants where the food was taking a while, I asked Inseon to teach me some Jeju-mal. I had loved the rich sounds and gentle intonations she had used on the phone with her mum.

At first, Inseon was reluctant. I doubt it'll do you much good when you travel to Jeju, she said. Everyone will be able to tell you're a mainlander. But when she saw that I was genuinely interested, she began to teach me the basics. I was most intrigued by the unfamiliar conjugations. When we attempted short conversations and I used the wrong tense out of hada – haen – hamen – hajaen, Inseon corrected me with a smile.

People say our word endings are short because we have such strong winds on Jeju, she said one day. The sound of the wind clips our words.

These were my impressions of Inseon's hometown – an unadorned language of abrupt word endings, a girlish grandmother who loved to watch basketball when she longed to be around people – at least until that evening towards the end of the year, after I'd quit my job, when we met up purely as friends for the first time.

That night, we had a late dinner at a noodle shop whose windows looked out on to a two-lane road that was nearly empty of traffic. I remember the impending new year, the fact that we would soon be that much older, had been weighing heavily on us at the time.

It's snowing, said Inseon.

I bit off my noodles and turned to the window.

No, it's not, I said.

You'll see it when a car goes by.

Soon enough, a sedan drove past, its headlights shining in the dark, and revealed a flurry of snow coruscating like fine grains of salt.

Inseon set down her chopsticks and went outside. I kept eating, watching her through the window. I thought she needed to make a phone call, but she'd left her mobile on the table. Was she going to take pictures? She had left her camera behind too, but maybe she was thinking through how she would film the scene. She often did this when we were out together, which left me with one of two options. Either I could look on with curiosity as she captured whatever she was seeing through her camera lens, or I could make myself comfortable and wait around while my mind drifted to other things.

To my surprise, Inseon didn't come back for her camera. She stood outside, unflinching against the wind, both hands in the pockets of her faded jeans, her thin turtleneck revealing the slender contours of her shoulders and shoulder blades. Another taxi went by, its headlights gleaming on the snow sifting down. She looked like she had forgotten everything else in the world. Her unfinished bowl of noodles. Me. The date, the time, the place. When she finally came back inside, I noticed the dusting of snow that had fallen on her head, the way it melted in the brief span it took her to walk over to our table and clung like beads of rain to her hair.

We finished our food in silence. When you've known someone a good while, you intuit when it's best not to speak. Eventually, after we had both set down our chopsticks and sat through a long pause, she began to tell me about the time she ran away from home as a teenager and nearly died. I was surprised. I knew how deeply Inseon cared for her mother, especially as she was widowed when Inseon was only nine and had raised her by herself until Inseon left for college.

You always describe your mum as a halmoni, so I thought your relationship with her was like the one I have with my grandmum, I said. But of course there's a difference between how I see my grandmother and my parents. With grandparents, things tend to be more straightforward . . . My grandmum's a giver, just giving and giving without end.

Inseon agreed, smiling gently. She was exactly like that, my mum, she said. She really treated me like I was her grandchild. Never pressured or scolded me about anything. Her tone was careful, as if her mother were right next to us listening.

I have no bones to pick about my childhood either, she continued. Both my parents were naturally soft-spoken, so our house was always calm. It got quieter still after my father died. I always felt like there was no one else in the world but the two of us – me and my mum. I used to get stomach pains at night sometimes, and my mum would tie a string round my thumb and prick my finger right beneath the nail, then rub my belly all night long. Aieee, my little sorghum-straw daughter. Nerves of silk, just like your daddy . . . she would sigh to herself.

Inseon stirred her broth with her chopsticks, realized she'd finished her noodles and set the chopsticks down on the table. She lined them up side by side as if someone would inspect them.

But that year . . . I don't know why, but I hated my mother so much that year, she said.

⁓

There were days I couldn't stand the burning sensation that climbed up my throat from the pit of my stomach. I hated the house. I hated the road I had to walk more than a half-hour from that backwoods house to get to the bus stop, and I hated the school where that bus dropped me off. I hated the sound of the school bell, the bars of 'Für Elise' that announced class was starting. I hated class, I hated the other kids who didn't seem to hate anything as much as I did, and I hated the school uniform I had to wear every day and wash and iron every weekend.

At some point I started hating my mum. She just sickened me, like every other nauseating thing. I despised her the way I despised myself. I despised

the food she made for me, hated watching her pains-
takingly wipe down our scuffed floor table or wear
her greying hair in a matronly bun, and loathed
seeing how she walked with a stoop like some whipping girl. My hatred grew until I could hardly
breathe. It was like I had this red-hot ball of rage
seething endlessly in my gut.

I finally walked out because I wanted to live. I
felt like if I didn't leave, that rage would kill me. I
changed into my school uniform as soon as I woke
up, packed underwear and socks instead of textbooks
and notebooks in my bookbag, then regular clothes
instead of my PE uniform in a separate canvas bag.
It was around this time of the year, late December.
My mum was leaving the village every morning at
dawn to help harvest and pack mandarins on other
orchards. As I nibbled at the food she had covered in
a cloth and left out for me, I looked around the house
for places where I might find some money. There was
a good amount of cash in the biscuit tin under the
TV where my mum kept the utility bills. That was
the money she'd made selling the mandarins from
our own harvest.

Before I left the house, I remember looking back
at the room where my mother slept. The sliding door
was open, the duvet neatly folded, but the electric

blanket and cotton mattress were spread out on the floor. I knew she kept a coping saw beneath the mattress. My mum believed the superstition that lying down to sleep over sharp metal warded off nightmares. Yet even with the saw under her mat, she was often plagued by bad dreams. Her breath would catch and she would shudder, or she would yowl like a wild cat as she sobbed. Seeing her like that, hearing the sounds she made, was hell for me. I swore then that I wouldn't regret leaving, that I would never come back. I wouldn't let that person darken my life any longer. With her stooped back and her feeble voice. The weakest, most cowardly person in the world.

I changed into my regular clothes in the restroom at the ferry terminal, then bought a ticket to Wando and took off. From Mokpo, I caught the express bus to Seoul and arrived well into the night. I booked a cheap room near the bus terminal, and I remember feeling anxious no matter how many times I checked the locks on the door. I baulked when I found strands of someone else's hair on the bed sheets, and even after I had wiped them away with wads of wet tissue, I slept curled up in a ball. As if I could protect myself from the filth that way.

The next day, I went out and called my niece

who was living in Seoul. I must have told you about her before, my mum's older sister's granddaughter — she's in Australia now. My aunt died early, but, unlike my mum, she married and had kids young, so my cousin is old enough to be my mother, and her daughter is two years older than me. I got scolded by the grown-ups if I just called her unni, so ever since I was little I awkwardly called her my niece unni.

My niece unni was a first-year in college at the time. She answered my call and told me to meet her in the lobby of the Jongno district YMCA. Luckily, she kept my trust and didn't show up with any adults in tow, but the moment she saw me, she started laying into me. She asked what on earth I was doing and told me to hurry home. Shouldn't I at least finish high school? Had I called my mother? Did I have the money to get back? Where was I staying? I tore out of there without saying a word. I had asked her to keep quiet, but I knew she would be telling everyone that day.

On my way back to my lodgings, I swore to myself. That I would do the opposite of everything my niece unni had said. I wouldn't call my mum, no way would I go back to the island, and I wasn't going to graduate from high school. The first thing I had to do was find a job. I spotted a Help Wanted ad posted outside a Japanese restaurant near the bus terminal and went in for an interview. Trembling inside the whole time, I lied and said I was on a leave of absence after my first year at the nearby teachers' college and, surprisingly, the restaurant owner didn't question me. He put me in an apron, set me to work waiting tables for two hours, then told me I could officially start the next day.

I left the restaurant, teeming with excitement on the walk back. With each step I took, the crowds on the streets seemed to part for me, saying, Come — from this moment on you only need to move forward. Even as one side of my chest was constricted with anxiety, my mind was as sharp as if I had icy water raining on my head. I remember thinking, Is this what they mean by freedom? Night was falling fast and, though my mid-length coat would have been sufficiently warm back in Jeju, the Seoul chill burrowed itself deep inside the folds. I had turned up my collar to keep out the biting wind when I slipped on an embankment coated in thin ice and snow. I remember how the emptiness felt against my feet as I fell. There's nothing beneath me. No ground. I'm going to die, I thought. Later I would learn that it had been a five-metre drop.

They said I was discovered around noon the

following day. There was a construction dig site beneath the embankment, and it just so happened that ownership of the site, where construction had been stalled since the summer, had recently transferred to a new owner who was visiting with the estate agent that day. They were terrified, thinking they had come across a dead body. They were even more stunned to find that I was still breathing.

I'd fallen on a heap of construction fabric meant for groundwater drainage. That was what had spared me. By some stroke of luck, I hadn't broken any bones either, but my head had absorbed the shock. I spent ten days in a nearby hospital, unidentified and unconscious, before I briefly came to. When I did, the nurse asked my name and I apparently answered, but I don't remember that at all. All I remember is that my niece unni was sitting at my bedside, her eyes blood red. I blacked out again, and the next time I woke, my mum was sitting there instead. The hospital room was dark except for a night light, but my mum's coal-black eyes seemed to glow all on their own as she looked down at me.

Inseon, my mum said. Try to answer. Do you know who I am?

When I groaned 'mmm' in reply, my mother

didn't cry, didn't tell me off, didn't shout for a nurse. Instead, she started rambling. At some point, she had grabbed my hand tight, and her eyes were gleaming.

She told me she had known I was hurt. Even before the hospital got in touch with her, she'd known. She'd seen me in a dream the night I fell from the embankment. I was five years old and sitting in a field of snow, but the snow that landed on my cheeks wouldn't melt. Even in her dream, that sight made her tremble in fear. Because why would snow not melt on a baby's warm face?

～

I heard that story before I met Inseon's mother in person. Ten years later, not long after Inseon moved back to Jeju, I was also on the island attending a training session for work. When I managed to find some time in my schedule one evening to take a taxi to Inseon's house, I was surprised to see her mother, who I'd heard was in the early stages of dementia, looking unexpectedly kempt and collected. Unlike Inseon, she was rather short, with delicate features and a lovely voice that made her seem like a young girl at heart. Enjoy your visit, she told me right before I stepped out of her room, quietly holding my hands.

Later, in the kitchen, Inseon said, She becomes more lucid when she meets strangers, maybe because she's nervous. She's always hated being a burden. She only cries and gets cross and acts like a child around me. A lot of the time, she mistakes me for her older sister.

The next day as I boarded the plane to Seoul, I thought back on that winter years ago when I'd first heard the story about Inseon running away from home. Strangely, I had come to feel as sorry for Inseon as I had for her mother. A girl of only seventeen — how deeply must she have hated herself and the world to despise someone so slight? Someone who slept on a saw. Who ground her teeth and sobbed through nightmares. Who spoke in a frail voice and constantly made herself small.

~

We left the noodle shop and walked the streets in silence. The snow clung desolately to the thick strands of Inseon's hair, as I'm sure it did to mine.

As we rounded another corner, a white untrodden road would open ahead of us like pages in a
giant picture book. The sounds of our feet
crunching over the snow, our parka sleeves
brushing against our sides and the shutters on the
shopfronts closing in the distance were all
resoundingly clear in the stillness. White steam
poured from our mouths and noses. Snowflakes
landed on the bridges of our noses and our lips.
They were quick to melt on our warm faces, and
new, startlingly cold crystals settled over their
wet traces. Neither of us seemed to be thinking
about the separate paths we would have to take to
get home. As we kept walking away from the
subway station like lovers who choose a roundabout route to delay their brief goodbyes, as we
traversed the hushed pedestrian crossings that
appeared round every corner like yet another
page in that book, I waited. For Inseon to break
the silence and continue her story.

*The night I was released from hospital and went
back to Jeju with my mum, she brought up the snow
again. Not as she'd seen it in her dream so much as*

the real events that had given rise to the dream. I wasn't fully recovered, but she lay beside me through the night and held me by the wrist as if she were worried I'd have the strength to run away again, startling and grabbing on tight again whenever she accidentally let go in her sleep.

She told me about how, when she was young, soldiers and police had murdered everyone in her village. My mum had been in her last year of elementary school and my aunt was seventeen. The two of them had been away on an errand at a distant cousin's house, which was how they managed to avoid the same fate. The next day, having heard the news, the sisters returned to the village and wandered the grounds of the elementary school all afternoon. Searching for the bodies of their father and mother, their older brother and eight-year-old sister. They looked over the bodies that had fallen every which way on top of one another and found that, overnight, a thin layer of snow had covered and frozen upon each face. They couldn't tell anyone apart because of the snow, and since my aunt couldn't bring herself to brush it away with her bare hands, she used a handkerchief to wipe each face clean. I'll wipe them, she told my mum, and you get a good look at them. She didn't want her little sister touching dead people.

But something about the words 'get a good look at them' so terrified my mum that all she could do was grab her sister's sleeve, shut her eyes tight and cling to her as they walked. Whenever my aunt said, Look at them, take a good look and tell me what you see, my mum reluctantly opened her eyes. That day, she came to understand something clearly. That when people died, their bodies went cold. Snow remained on their cheeks, and a thin layer of bloody ice set over their faces.

The following year, Inseon began to make documentary films in earnest as she had long been interested in doing. Later it occurred to me that the story she had told me that snowy night probably sprang from rough ideas she must have been sketching for future projects.

We were now retracing our steps towards the subway station, turning back the pages we had opened as we walked. My toes were freezing inside my drenched trainers. My fists, shoved deep inside the pockets of my parka, were numb with cold. The snow on Inseon's head was as thick as a white woollen hat, and with each word she spoke, her breath blazed out like gossamer flames in the dark.

‿

Until then, I'd had no idea. All I knew was that my grandparents on my mother's side were long gone and that my aunt's family were our only relatives, but I thought this was because my mum had just one sibling. I'm sure I wasn't the only kid to think this. Then and now, the grown-ups never talked about what had happened.

I think my mum brought it up that night in the grip of some sort of fervour. Or perhaps a chill – her jaw kept clattering like she was cold. I was at a loss, seeing her in such a different state from the quiet, sad grandmother-type I thought I knew so well. It wasn't clear in that moment if this sudden change had been brought on by the horror from decades earlier that she was relaying to her daughter for the first time, or by the shock of the accident that had almost robbed her of her child. Remarkably, though, she didn't say a word about my running away, not then and not after. She didn't blame me, and she didn't ask why. Just as she never spoke about how two young sisters managed to find their dead family and see to their burial, or what perseverance and good fortune was required for them to survive afterwards. She only spoke about the snow. As if there were a causal link between the unmelting snow she had seen decades before in reality and the snow on my face in her recent dream, and this link was the single most terrifying logic running through her life.

Then my mum said: The thing is, every time it snows, it comes back. I try not to think about it, but it keeps coming back. So in my dream that night, to see your face whited out by snow . . . as soon as I opened my eyes to the dawn, I thought, my baby's dead. Aieee, all I could think was that you were dead.

❤

Inseon told me this hadn't eased her ambivalence towards her mother. She remained conflicted afterwards, and in some ways felt more confused. But the loathing she had once found too excruciating to bear, even briefly, vanished that night as if it had never existed, and she said she no longer knew exactly what the object of the fire blazing in the pit of her stomach had been.

She never brought up that story again, let alone hinted at it, but whenever it snows like this, I remember her. The girl roaming the schoolyard, searching, well into the evening. A child of thirteen clinging to her seventeen-year-old sister as if her sister wasn't a child herself, hanging on by a sleeve, too scared to see but unable to look away.

⌒

The wipers are streaking across the bus windscreen, powerless against the pelting snow. As the blizzard thickens, the bus slows down. The driver's profile is tense as he peers ahead, his field of vision obscured. The tourist sitting behind the driver looks on edge too, as he stares out of the windscreen, chin in hand.

When I step off this bus, I'll have to plough my way through that snow. I'll have to trudge ahead, one unsteady step at a time, barely able to open my eyes in the gale winds.

Inseon would be used to this weather. If I were her . . .

I think of Inseon's self-assuredness, her tendency to not give up, to persist. I imagine what she would do in this situation.

If she were me, she would buy a lantern. Since if she couldn't transfer directly to the local bus and night had completely fallen by then, she'd have to walk up the unlit field paths. She would find rubber boots and a hand shovel too. Because, unlike the coastal roads, the roads through the uplands will be snowed under.

This is absurd, I mutter to myself. I'm not Inseon. Not only am I not used to this kind of weather, I've never experienced anything like it, and I certainly don't love that bird enough to make the trek to her house tonight in this storm.

⌒

I can tell we have finally entered P— when I see the signs for Nonghyup and the post office. I reach out and press the bell to signal my stop, and the bus slows to a halt. The wind outside seems to ease up then too, as if on cue. But no, on second glance, I see that the wind must have died down at some point along the way. I feel as if I've stepped into the eye of the storm. It's a little past four in the afternoon but so dim that it seems like another heavy storm is approaching.

The streets are lifeless. No passing cars on the road either. Only heavy snowflakes making their unfathomably slow descent. A traffic light glows bright red behind the dense arrangement of falling snow. The bus has driven on and sits stopped at the crossing, waiting on the signal to change. As the snow lands on the wet asphalt, each flake seems to falter for a moment. Then, like a trailing sentence at the close of a conversation, like the dying fall of a final cadence, like fingertips cautiously retreating before ever landing on a shoulder, the flakes sink into the slick blackness and are soon gone.

4

Birds

A few times on the bus ride over here, I'd noticed the winds die down as abruptly as they have now. Each time I'd assumed the weather conditions must have changed. Now I wonder if I was wrong. Maybe those areas didn't see much wind. If I were to return there at this moment would I be met with the same static calm and steady precipitation as here?

I hear the bus continue on its way, the sound of its engine muffled by snow. Wiping the flakes from my eyelashes, I try to find my bearings. This is the coastal road; other than the express buses, regular transit buses don't stop here. I have to remember where the bus stop by the intersection was, the one Inseon pointed out to me before as we drove down past it in her truck. Is it the junction I can see up ahead or the one behind me? At which of the two corners should I turn? I decide to walk ahead. I'm not worried about losing my way. I'm headed towards the large snow clouds shimmering over the uplands. If I don't see a bus stop from the corner, I can turn and walk back.

It is unbelievably quiet.

If not for the chill of the icy particles falling and settling on my forehead and on my cheeks, I might wonder if I'm dreaming. Are the streets empty because of the storm? Or are the lights out in the small shops selling cold seafood soup and noodles in anchovy broth because it's a Sunday? The metal chairs upended on tables and the pavement signs lying toppled behind locked doors have an air of disuse, and suggest that these establishments have been closed for some time. The business selling outdoor goods under a shoddy front sign is shuttered. Mannequins wear flimsy autumn clothes behind one window, through which I glimpse cloth the colour of rice draped over a long rack of clothes. The one place with its lights on in this silent little town is a tiny corner shop.

I need to find a lantern and a hand shovel. The corner shop might not carry what I'm looking for, but I can ask them to point me in the right direction. If I'm lucky, someone might even loan me what I need. I can also ask where I might catch the bus for Inseon's village. But as I head towards the shop, the lights go dark. A middle-aged man, presumably the owner, walks out in his jacket. Seeing him wrap a chain round the handles of the glass doors and turn the padlock with practised ease, I quicken my steps.

Wait, I call out.

But the man is climbing into a mini truck parked out front. I start running, wiping the snow away from my eyelids as best I can.

Please – wait!

The countless crystals soak up and erase my voice. I hear the truck start, the sound stifled by the wintry calm. The vehicle backs up on to the empty road. I wave my arms at the driver. Then look on helplessly as the truck speeds away.

~

I've stopped running. I walk, feeling a strange compulsion to match my steps to the pace of the drifting snow, which itself seems synchronized to the passage of time. Reaching the intersection where the truck made a right turn and disappeared off in the direction of the port, I look up towards where I'm headed, in the uplands. The small signpost I spot in the distance — is that the stop I'm looking for?

I walk to the other side of the crossing, over which snow is falling thick and fast and melting away just as quickly on the black, wet asphalt. After about fifty metres, I discover that the signpost is in fact a bus-stop marker. There is no shelter; no bus numbers or route information are indicated. There is only a small bus icon on an aluminium sign, clinging to the metal post under the streaming sky.

⌣

As I head towards the bus stop, I pray the weather will clear up now that the winds have calmed. But the snowfall only grows heavier. A seemingly limitless cascade of whiteness is generated out of the ashen air.

As a child, I read that ultra-fine particles of dust or ash had to be present for a snowflake to form. And that clouds were not only made of suspended water droplets but were full of dust and ash that rose from the ground with water vapour. When two water molecules bind together in the clouds to form that initial snow crystal, it is these specks of dust that form the nucleus of the snowflake. The crystals are hexagonal in shape because of how a water molecule arranges itself, and as they fall, they continue to bind with other snow crystals in their path. If the distance between the clouds and the ground were infinite, the snow-flakes too would grow to infinity, but in reality their descent never lasts for longer than an hour. Snowflakes are feather-light, thanks to the empty spaces between the many branches generated by their countless bindings. And it is these spaces within the crystal that absorb and trap sounds, dampening the acoustics of its surroundings. As its multiple surfaces reflect light in myriad direc-tions, the snowflake appears colourless, appears white.

I remember the images of snow crystals that accompanied these explanations. The book was bound with thin interleaving sheets of glassine to protect the colour plates. I had turned the trans-lucent paper to find a page filled with variously shaped snow crystals. Their intricacy over-whelmed me. Some of the crystals had smooth hexagonal columns instead of symmetrical plates, and the tiny captions beneath explained that, on the boundary of snow and rain, snowflakes took these elongated forms. For weeks and months afterwards, I had pictured those delicate, silvery columns whenever I saw sleet. On days of heavy snowfall, I used to extend my coat sleeve to watch the flakes settle on the fluff on its dark fabric and dissolve. It made me dizzy to consider the innumerable combinations of coruscating hexagonal crystals like the ones I'd seen in the book that made up each grain of snow. For days after, I had woken from sleep and, while my eyes remained closed, imagined it was still snowing outside. I had seen snow drift down around me indoors while I lay sprawled on the floor, working on some tedious holiday assignment. Flakes landing on my hand, from which I'd just removed a hangnail. Flakes landing on the loose hairs and eraser dust strewn across the floor.

The strangest thing, snow, I recall Inseon saying. Had she been picturing scenes similar to the ones I'd imagined? *How does something like that fall from the sky?* she'd said, eyes directed not at me but at the window, as though she were quietly disputing someone outside, someone invisible. As though she found it difficult to accept its beauty. I remember how she told me, that night in late December as the year was winding down, *Whenever it snows like this, I remember her. The girl roaming the schoolyard, searching, well into the evening.*

Her hair as she said this had been covered in a thick layer of snow. It looked like she was wearing a white woollen hat. My hands were stiff and numb inside the pockets of my parka. We had walked, a sound like that of crumbling salt trailing behind us with each step. *The thing is, every time it snows, it comes back. I try not to think about it, but it keeps coming back.*

⁓

I startle as I reach the bus stop.

I had thought it deserted, but there's an elderly woman who looks to be well over eighty standing by the signpost. Her back is bent and she has a cane. A light grey woollen hat is pulled over her short white hair, and her quilted coat matches her hat. On her feet are dark rubber shoes lined with fake fur. She looks over at me as I approach, tilting her tremulous head to one side. I nod in greeting, but she goes on staring.

Wondering if she missed my gesture, I bow again, and notice a hint of a smile briefly flit across her small lined face.

I didn't see her at first as she was standing beneath heavily snow-laden trees. Her light hat and coat are effective camouflage in this landscape. It's strange. I don't recall seeing this much snow cover on any of the trees we passed during the hour-long drive along the coast. The fierce winds whipped the lighter snow away before it had a chance to settle. Now that it's falling thick and fast, a few minutes in this calm is all it takes for the precipitation to accumulate on the branches.

I turn to the empty intersection behind me, following the woman's gaze. I stand next to her and observe her profile until she slowly turns her head towards me. Empty, dispassionate, her eyes briefly meet mine. The look is neither friendly nor indifferent, nor is it cold — in fact, it leans towards muted warmth. I realize that she reminds me of Inseon's mother. In her small frame and dainty features, but most of all in her air of indifference mingled with subdued kindness.

I'm not sure I should speak to her.

I imagine Inseon would have easily struck

up a conversation. The first time she and I travelled together for work, we visited a few regions for a feature on some of the more renowned mountains and the scenery of the surrounding villages. Wherever we went, Inseon was quick to bond with the older women. She had no qualms about asking for directions, sharing food with strangers and enquiring around to find someone to put us up for the night. When I asked what her secret was, she said it might have something to do with her being raised by a mother who was older than most.

I think about how the majority of her films feature women of a certain age, women who are often addressed as halmoni. I always assumed Inseon's outgoing nature would have played a large part in generating the extraordinary intimacy of her interviews. That as the women paused in their remarks or trailed off into silence when their eyes fell on the camera, Inseon would have sat across from them, her face open and sincere, and tried her best to meet their gaze.

It was this off-screen face of hers I pictured while watching her documentary on Việt Nam, specifically the scene where the local guide is translating Inseon's questions to the woman who lives alone in a remote jungle village.

She is asking if you have a story you want to tell her about that night.

Above the somewhat stiffly translated subtitles, the woman looks past the camera. Her short white hair is tucked behind her ears, her face small and gaunt, and her eyes are unusually sharp.

This person came here from Korea to ask you this.

Finally, the woman speaks.

All right. I'll tell you.

She stares steadily at the camera with remarkable focus, not once glancing at the interpreter. The gleam in her eyes pierced the lens and – I imagined – Inseon's eyes, lancing directly into my own. This was the reply of someone who had waited a very long time for this moment. This brief consent, I realized, held the entire weight of her life.

⌣

The layer of snow on the woman's hat grows thick. Her eyes are on the intersection, which remains quiet. The only movement around us is the downward progression of the thick wet snow.

I gather up my nerve and speak to her.

Samchun, I say.

Inseon had told me to address older people here as samchun. *Only outsiders say ajossi or ajumoni, halmoni or haraboji, she said. If you start off by calling them samchun, even if you can't string together a sentence in Jeju-mal, they're likely to be less guarded, thinking you've lived on the island for a good while.*

Have you been waiting long? I ask.

The woman turns her blank eyes towards me.

Is there a bus coming soon?

Slowly, she lifts one hand from the cane she's leaning on. She points at her ear, eyes twinkling. Then shakes her head from side to side, as a wan smile unfolds over her face. Her thin lips, which I thought would never part, open at last.

With all this snow . . .

Her head continues to tremble as she turns away, as if to say she won't be making further conversation. She casts her eyes to the distance, towards where the bus is yet to appear.

∿

I note the resemblance to Inseon's mother again, and for some reason my heart sinks.

Enjoy your visit, Inseon's mother had said to

me with a similarly apprehensive air, even as she spoke in a clear Seoul-mal. And with the dispassion that marks people who have long suffered and been tempered by anguish. An equanimity that signals their readiness to withstand whatever misfortune might still be in store, all while remaining vigilant, even in the face of joy and goodwill.

I wondered who she had mistaken me for. Later that night Inseon would tell me how her mother frequently forgot that she had a daughter and sometimes lapsed into childishness, taking Inseon for her own older sister. Hearing this, I wondered if she'd assumed I was a friend or acquaintance of her sister's. My use of Seoul-mal would have confused her then. When she smiled at me, her creased eyelids had nearly closed and the light in her eyes had dulled. Seeing her reach out her hands, I extended mine. We looked at each other, our four hands overlapping. She searched my face curiously, cautiously, as if to determine who I was. When she eventually let go of my hands with a gentle smile, I bowed and left the room. I found Inseon by the kitchen stove.

What are you making?

Bean juk, Inseon said without turning round. I mixed black beans with white beans. Half-half.

She began stirring the large pot with a long wooden paddle. I went to stand beside her, and finally she looked at me.

She needs protein but she can't digest anything else, so I make this for her.

Do you use the green-fleshed ones?

No, just black soya beans.

How many servings is this?

Usually I only make as much as we'll eat, but I've made more since you're here.

Wonderful, I said. My stomach's feeling a little unsettled as it happens.

This was true. I had mild spasms, possibly due to the flight, and the beginnings of a migraine, which usually accompanied the spasms.

Oh no. Inseon knitted her brows. Maybe coming here was too much.

No, I said, shaking my head. I wanted to add that I'd been meaning to visit for a while but felt awkward and said nothing. I watched the dark grey juk, flecked with black, thicken as Inseon went on patiently stirring.

It smells really good.

It tastes even better. Inseon smiled assuredly and switched off the gas.

Were you planning on using this? I asked,

pointing to a large bowl on a rack. She nodded. I put the bowl on a wooden tray and brought it over to her, and she ladled the juk out. It felt easy and familiar to stand over the kitchen sink and lend a hand, as if we really were sisters for whom this kind of wordless back-and-forth was second nature.

That's a generous serving.

You know the saying – a good appetite, a long life. My mum's going to live a good long life.

Inseon balanced the tray in her hands and headed to the main bedroom. I darted past her to open the door. Inseon stepped inside and closed the door behind her, leaving me to myself. I wandered about for a bit, then wiped the beautifully oiled dining table and laid two sets of spoons and chopsticks across from each other. I ladled the bean juk into two large bowls and placed them on the table. I pulled up the chair, sat down and stared at the steaming bowls.

By the time Inseon reappeared with the emptied bowl on her tray, the juk was barely steaming. Meeting my eyes, she grinned.

What are you grinning at?

Seeing you reminded me.

Of what?

Inseon placed the tray over the sink and sat across from me.

I told you before, right? About how I ran away in my second year of high school.

Sure.

And how my mum wouldn't let go of my hand and talked to me all night when I came home again from the hospital.

Inseon looked up at me briefly as if to ask if I remembered.

I remembered, of course. Though I was still straining to connect her mother as I'd imagined her based on Inseon's stories to the tiny halmoni I'd met earlier. I remembered her hands on mine, how warm they were as if she'd been keeping them under a blanket. Despite our clasped hands, I could tell she didn't fully trust me. As I'd sat and stared at the steaming juk, I'd wondered if I could have reassured her somehow. If I could have talked and acted in a more natural manner to convince her that this stranger who spoke the mainland tongue was in fact harmless and a friend of her sister's.

There's something I didn't tell you that day, something interesting, Inseon said with a smile. When I was hospitalized without a guardian, she says she saw me here, at home.

I don't understand, I said.

The hospital couldn't contact her of course, not until I came to and gave them my name. But my mum swears I was here the day before she got the call.

You mean in her dream? I asked after a long pause.

Inseon's cheeks puffed as she held back laughter.

She says she came out around midnight, switched the light on and saw me sitting at this table.

Okay, but dreams can be uncanny like that, can't they? I said with confusion.

I mean, after ten days of worrying about my whereabouts, I guess she could have experienced a temporary delirium.

So then what happened?

She made juk.

What?

She made juk for me.

Spirits eat juk?

Inseon and I chuckled together.

My mum had the same thought. She made the rice juk, praying I would at least taste it. Reasoning that if I was able to eat hot food, that would mean I wasn't dead. But she says I just sat and stared at the juk and wouldn't say a word. Like you were doing just now. Like you're too famished, too exhausted to even lift a spoon.

I'm really not that hungry or tired, I said.

Inseon picked up her spoon. I did the same and tried the bean juk. Despite what I had just claimed, as soon as the warm, nutty flavour filled my mouth I was overcome with hunger.

It's so good, I murmured, and, hearing this, Inseon said in her confident way, Have as much as you want. There's plenty more.

I ate in silence until the bowl was half empty. When I lifted my head, Inseon was quietly observing me. As an older sister might do. Feeling sheepish, I asked her, And so, did you?

Did I what? Inseon asked, then remembered our conversation and shook her head. No, I didn't eat the juk.

She pushed her chair back and stood up. Opening the fridge, she bent down to retrieve a large container of kimchi. Mum says I stared at the bowl like I couldn't take my eyes off it, she said. Says it was clear I was desperate to eat it, and so she felt quite sure I wasn't a ghost.

As Inseon set a plate of kimchi on the table, I

noticed that she looked more at peace than she had in Seoul. It can be difficult to distinguish for-bearance from resignation, sorrow from partial reconciliation, fortitude from loneliness. I thought about how difficult it can be to tell these emotions apart on the basis of facial expressions and gestures, about how the person in question may struggle to distinguish these feelings in themselves.

Mum retold that story all winter, Inseon said. For a while, I think she brought it up every time we sat down to eat. You came to see your umung that night, didn't you, gasinae, she'd say, know-ing a bowl of my juk would bring you back?

⌒

The elderly woman stares at a set of traffic lights at the intersection. The flakes falling before them glow a different shade as the signals change. Only four buses have passed by us so far, all coastal-route buses headed in both directions. No one seems to have got on or off the buses; I don't recall hearing any of them pull to a stop.

How could it be this quiet?

The sea that runs alongside the one-hour

stretch of coastal road had churned and frothed as if to engulf the island, the waves advancing from all sides, crests white with spume, to crash into the jetty and erupt into air.

Could a storm die down so abruptly?

The snow is falling at an even slower pace now. As though in inverse proportion to the speed of its descent, the snow grows dense, the flakes larger and crowding closer together. Every time I remove my gloves to wipe my eyelids, the rims of my eyes grow wet. Everything within sight turns blurry, lambent. I bend down to brush the snow off my trainers and feel its cold wetness seep through my ankle socks.

If the temperature were a few degrees higher, the snow would have swamped the island. Like the torrential downpour in Inseon's footage from a decade ago, a merciless rain inundating the dense tropical forest of Việt Nam.

That August, after returning from her trip, Inseon had holed up at home to edit. I dropped by one day and she showed me the rain scene for the first time. We sat next to each other in front of the monitor and, as we watched, claps of thunder and the sudden rat-a-tat of a cloudburst could be heard outside, until I couldn't tell where the rainstorm over the jungle in Việt Nam ended and the heavy shower over the streets of Seoul began. Exotic, unfamiliar flowers and thick tropical leaves shook and deflected the teeming rain. A muddy ditch appeared and wound its way across the village centre like a river. Women with trousers rolled up to their thighs hurried across the yard to scoop the drowning chicks and chickens into bamboo baskets. The shot lasted a good ten minutes and affected me profoundly. As I sat in silence, Inseon began to describe the tropical heat she'd experienced.

Forty degrees Celsius seemed to be the tipping point, she said. I'd walk outside the hostel and see hundreds of dark moths packed over mud walls, trying to evade the heat. The temperature on those days always rose into the forties. And all sorts of unusual insects would appear. The kind you don't usually see, and they looked different too — big and dazzling as they crawled out and scuttled over the scorching ground — and you just knew, instinctively, that they were deadly. On those days, when it rained, it came down in gallons, just endless buckets of water. But the day I shot this, the rain was even heavier than usual. It didn't let up for two days and two nights.

Once she had a rough cut, Inseon invited a few close acquaintances to a pre-release screening. In this version the rainstorm scene followed shots of the woman's daily life, the woman who had looked at the camera and answered, All right. I'll tell you. We saw her walk to the yard to wash her kettle at the water pump. She pumped the handle a few times to get the water flowing, then rinsed the kettle inside and out. On the fourth rinse, we heard her low voice say as subtitles appeared on screen, *That night the soldiers came.* Before her account was over, the long-take scene of falling rain began. The grass-thatched roofs were drenched. The brass water pump gleamed as it deflected the pelting raindrops. The overgrown hedge of wild jasmine shook. The chicken coop was awash with muddy water and flapping wings. Women appeared in dripping, rolled-up cotton trousers, bamboo baskets over their heads. The yard, choppy with rainwater. The round heads of chicks, wobbling like wet balls of wool.

～

The single flake that settled and melted over my glove just now was as close to a pristine six-armed snow crystal as one is likely to find. The one that settles next to it is partly crumbled, but the remaining four branches retain their delicate shape. These soft, deteriorating dendrites are the first to melt away. The tiny white centre, the part that resembles a grain of salt, lingers for a breath before dissolving.

People say 'light as snow'. But snow has its own heft, which is the weight of this drop of water.

People say 'light as a bird'. But birds too have their weight.

The feeling of Ama's two feet on my right shoulder, rough against the weft of my pullover. The warm softness of Ami's chest as he perched on my left index finger. Strange, the sensation of contact with a living thing, how it can remain imprinted on the skin. As if touch alone can singe and break flesh. The delicate press of those birds against my skin remains unmatched.

How are they this light? I had asked, but Inseon shook her head. She told me bird bones were hollow and that this might be what made them lighter. Their largest organs are their air sacs, she added, which resemble balloons.

Birds eat so little because their tiny stomachs

really can't hold much, she continued. Plus they've only got small quantities of blood and body fluids, so losing just a few drops of blood or not having water to drink for a short while can be fatal. Even the trace amount of toxicity in a gas flame can pollute their blood, which is why I changed to an electric stove.

Inseon lowered her voice as if she thought the birds might actually understand her. Honestly I've sometimes regretted taking them in, she said. You don't have to be as cautious with cats or dogs.

The birds flew up from my hand and shoulder. There was a brief beating of wings, then they settled again, Ama on Inseon's shoulder and Ami on the windowsill overlooking the yard. I felt a lingering buoyant sensation where Ama and Ami had each pushed off as they'd leaped into the air. A sensation similar to soap suds or foam on skin.

How much do they weigh? I asked.

Inseon turned to look Ama in the eyes.

I'm not sure. Maybe twenty grams?

For some reason, a human foetus came to mind. I'd heard a long while ago that a foetus weighs about twenty grams around the time you can hear the beating of its still-developing heart. At that stage, the curled-up foetus is almost indistinguishable from a bird embryo in its egg.

The next morning, the ever-hospitable Inseon drove me to the airport in her truck. Back in Seoul, on nights when I had trouble sleeping, I went online to read about birds. I came across an article in a popular science magazine that described birds as extant dinosaurs. While the Earth's surface burned and boiled in the aftermath of an asteroid collision and the volcanic ash that covered the atmosphere decimated animals and plants alike, the article said that feathered dinosaurs, or birds, were one organism that managed to survive the devastation by flying for months on end. Later I found a website where most currently living birds were catalogued with photos and nomenclature. I read the taxonomic names out loud, names I was unlikely to remember, but this helped to pass the time. On another night, I happened across an anatomical diagram of a bird done in clear lines, which I found especially beautiful and was moved to save on my computer. I saw the balloon-like air sacs Inseon had described, saw how the bones were full of oval holes and resembled wind instruments. *So that's what made them so light*, I murmured to myself in the dark, recalling the roughness of Ama's feet against the fabric of my pullover.

~

A giant snowflake settles on the back of my hand. It has travelled more than a thousand metres from the clouds. How many times it must have fused and combined as it descended to have grown to this size. And yet how light it is. I try to picture a twenty-gram snowflake, its vastness.

I look over at the woman. She remains as still as a stone figure, hands folded on her cane. How long has she been waiting like this? How are her bare hands not freezing? Time, it seems, is barely passing. It feels like we are the last living, breathing beings in this silent town with its shuttered and empty shops. I repress a sudden urge to lean across and wipe the snow from her grey lashes. A strange fear grips me. A fear that the instant I touch her, not only her face but her entire body might scatter and vanish into the snowy landscape.

~

You have to keep an eye on them even when they look fine.

Birds will pretend like nothing's wrong, no matter how much pain they're in. They instinctively endure and hide pain to avoid being targeted by predators. By the time they fall off their perch, it's too late.

While Inseon spoke with deep concern, Ama had remained on her shoulder. Her white face was turned towards me, but I knew she was probably looking back at Inseon with one eye and following her own shadow on the wall with the other. That shadow was part of Inseon's shadow, which was twice as big as Inseon herself. Amused, I found a pencil from a case in my bag and walked over to the wall.

I'll erase it later if you don't like it.

Inseon sat still for me while I traced a faint outline of her giant shadow from the head to the shoulder, and of the equally large black contour of the bird. Ami fluttered up from the windowsill and settled on the shade of the lamp above the dining table. As the light swayed, the shadows swayed with it. When the lampshade stopped moving, the shadows settled right back inside the line I'd drawn.

No, no.

Ami sighed from the lampshade. He must have picked up the word from his unwitting human companion. I wondered when and in what circumstances Inseon would have uttered that word.

Petting Ama's head, Inseon said, It's bedtime for you both.

She started singing, as if this were the signal between them. I didn't know the song, but the melody was familiar enough. A lullaby, though I couldn't follow the words as they were in dialect. Before Inseon reached the end of the first bar, Ama started humming along in an offbeat round. An extraordinarily serene if subtly dissonant harmony threaded the air. Ami remained quiet, as if he were listening to the song. Though his face was towards me, he was probably following Inseon and Ama's swaying shadow with one eye, and the tree out in the yard shivering in the evening light with the other. What was it like to live with two fields of vision? I wondered. Maybe it was like this out-of-time round for two voices. Or like living a dream and reality at once.

I feel the line of pain reactivate, starting in the eyes and extending past the nape of the neck and stiff shoulders to my stomach. I'd spat out the chewing gum earlier on the bus when it lost its sweetness. I doubt gum would help now.

I remove my gloves. Rub my palms together until they feel warm and press them to my lids and around my eyes. Squat a few times, bending my knees. Rotate my shoulders and neck. Straighten my back. Take deep breaths. Walk three steps forward and three steps back, returning to my place beside the woman each time. If I'm able to run a hot bath in time, I could still ward off the spasms. If I get some warm juk in my stomach and find a snug place to relax and stretch my body.

If only Inseon were at home now and not in that hospital in Seoul. If only she were here to answer my call in surprise and come pick me up in her truck. If only she were here to say to me, as I sit in the passenger seat massaging my eyes, *Remember how my bean juk made you feel all better? Let's go and make some.* Her eyes smiling in that assured way she has.

The glow of the traffic light brightens. The snow takes on deeper hues of red, yellow and green as it falls past the signal. Evening is settling in.

It seems the bus isn't coming after all.

Even if one were to pull up now, once we got to Inseon's village it would be too dark for me to find my way.

It's time to get on a coastal-route bus and head to Seogwipo to find a bed for the night. If there's a pharmacy that opens on Sundays, I can get some Tylenol at least and hope it will tide me over. If that doesn't work, I can find a hospital tomorrow morning, and if I'm lucky I might even get a prescription for the one migraine medication that works for me.

But first I have to call her, I mutter out loud. My breath wafts into the falling snow. I reconsider. No, I should text. She can't really answer her phone. The moment it vibrates, she might be having her fingers pierced with needles again.

The lacerating pain in my eyes grows acute. Knowing it won't make a difference, I reach into my pocket for some gum. I pop two from the blister pack and start chewing. Nausea hits me immediately and I spit them back out, into the paper napkin I received on the plane along with a cup of water. A sticky liquid oozes out as I wrap the gum in the beige paper.

I change my mind again. It's best to call. It would be harder for her to reposition herself to tap out a message. If she can't handle the phone herself, her carer can hold it up for her. And I should be able to make out every staticky word Inseon whispers into the phone in the quiet of this place.

I have to tell her I'm giving up. That there's a snowstorm, that I'm ill. Inseon knows how abruptly my migraines can come on. And how the abdominal spasms that inevitably follow knock me out for several days. As for the severity of the snow and its impact on transport here, I hardly need to tell her.

⁓

After the fifth ring, I end the call. I wait a full minute before pressing the call button again. My phone is long overdue for a replacement and this is all it takes for the battery to drop to one bar.

Finally, a connection. Inseon, I call out, my ear straining to hear her whispering voice. Instead, I hear a woman's urgent voice say, Later, call back later.

The line goes dead. I stare at the screen. It must be the carer. I could hear a general commotion surrounding her voice, a bustle of noise that didn't seem to belong to a patient room.

I can't figure out what's happening. The battery's charge is down to ten per cent. I'll have to recharge it before I can make another call. I need to get to Seogwipo.

Loosening my tight grip on the phone, I slip it into my pocket and glance at the woman beside me. If the buses have stopped running, shouldn't I tell her before I go? Won't she need my help given that she's hard of hearing and uses a cane?

The woman goes on staring at the intersection, seemingly oblivious. To get her attention, I'll have to touch her. I'm about to tap her on the shoulder when her face changes. Her eyes glint even as they remain steady. I follow her gaze and, unbelievably, a small bus is turning into the intersection, its roof buried under a thick layer of snow.

I hear the engine as the bus approaches, though the snow soon absorbs the dull reverberations. The bus grinds to a stop with a sound that reminds me of chalk on a blackboard. That ringing too is muffled by the placid snow.

The front door opens. Damp heated air rushes out and reaches my nose. The driver, who has one cotton-gloved hand on the gear lever, addresses the woman.

Were you waiting long?

He is wearing tortoiseshell glasses and a dark navy uniform and looks to be in his early forties.

Two buses got stuck uphill in the snow. You've been waiting all this time in the freezing cold, have you?

As earlier, the woman points to her ear and nods without answering. Using her cane, she slowly climbs on to the bus, and I follow behind as if in a trance. The bus is carrying no one else.

Are you going to Secheon-ri? I ask before tapping my transit card on the reader.

Yes, that's right, the driver says politely in Seoul-mal, and I sense a distancing in his changed tone.

Could you let me know when we're in Secheon-ri?

Where exactly? he asks. We stop four times in Secheon-ri alone. It's a big village.

I can't recall the name of the bus stop nearest Inseon's place. I only remember that it was an unfamiliar sounding Jeju word.

The driver stares at me as I hesitate. I can hear the squeak and swish of the wipers as they clear the snow off the windscreen.

This bus usually runs until nine, but there won't be another one today, he says.

I still can't answer.

I'm telling you this is the last bus going into Secheon today, the driver explains, seeing that I don't speak Jeju-mal and he has misgivings about my general attire and appearance given the weather. I thank him.

I don't know the name of the stop, but I'll recognize it when we get there. I'll let you know.

Unconvinced by my own words, I tap my card. I sit behind the woman, who leans on her short cane for support. The snow on her hat has already melted into droplets beading the napped wool.

What I said to the driver isn't entirely a lie.

At the bus stop nearest Inseon's place — which is still a thirty-minute hike away — there's a large hackberry tree that must be about five hundred years old. I remember too the location of a tiny front-room shop that sells beverages and cigarettes. As long as it isn't pitch-black by the time we get there, as long as there's a hint of twilight left, surely I can't miss such a big tree.

No matter what's happening to Inseon right now, my best course of action is to head to her place. To charge my phone once I get there and then to call her. Of course this is what she would most want from me too.

I feel I've lucked out. I managed to fly in on the last flight to Jeju, and I just caught the last bus to Inseon's village. I think about the couple on the plane. *You call this lucky? Are you seeing this weather?*

Could good luck be carrying me headlong into danger?

I lean my head against the cold window and bear the pain of my eyes being gouged by a dull blade. As ever, pain isolates me. I am trapped in the torturous moments my own body generates second by second. I am dislodged from the time prior to pain, from the world of the not-ill.

If only I could lie down somewhere warm.

I picture the large bedroom at Inseon's, which she let me use last autumn. The bedding was folded to one side as if the owner meant to return shortly. The scent of fabric softener suggested she had washed the blankets for me, and they felt crisp and dry and cosy against my skin. That first day I slept unusually soundly in my warm cocoon before waking up around midnight. On a sudden whim I looked under the floor mattress and found the rusted coping saw, which I imagined had lain dormant there for a very long time.

Dusk is rapidly setting in. The bus passes through the bank of grey-white snow clouds and mist I'd seen all the way from the coastal road. The houses dotted along the road are now gone. Snowy deciduous trees stretch out on either side in a seemingly vast woodland.

The bus slows to a stop. The woman gets up

from her seat. She hasn't indicated or told the driver where she's headed, but the driver seems to know where to let her off. Perhaps he's familiar with the residents here from driving the same route every day. The woman walks to the rear door, cane tapping as she goes. She tilts her tremulous head to glance back at me with an expression I can't make out — is it a faint smile, a parting salute, or simply a vacant look? — before turning away.

Should he be letting people off in such a deserted spot? I look around and glimpse a low wall of porous black rocks through the trees. A house. There's a footpath trailing between two of these snow-covered walls. Perhaps it leads to a village. The driver waits for the woman to set both feet firmly down on the snowy ground before closing the door. Her stooped figure trudges through the heavy snow and gradually recedes. I shift in my seat to follow her until she is out of sight. I don't understand it. She is neither kin nor acquaintance. She's only a stranger I happened to stand beside at a bus stop. Why then do I feel in turmoil, as if I've just bid someone farewell?

The bus slowly continues up the gentle slope

for another five minutes, then stops. The driver turns off the engine, pulls the handbrake. Please wait while I chain the tyres, he shouts.

A blustery wind blows in through the front door of the bus as the driver steps down. As my migraine worsens, my mind goes numb, until the parting and the woman recede from memory. Any apprehensions or thoughts about the bird I must save, my concern for Inseon – all ebb outside the sharp boundary carved out by the pain.

I see that it has got even darker and that the wind rushing in through the open door is growing turbulent. The blizzard is about to resume. It's almost as if the calm that's surrounded us since the bus stop in P— emanated from the woman herself, and now that she's gone, it too has retreated.

The woods shudder and cry out. Snow topples from trees in great flurries. My forehead feels like it's about to shatter. I lean against the window and recall the storm I saw earlier on the coastal road. Cloud banks dispersing in the far horizon as snow sweeps over the water's surface like huge flocks of birds. The grey sea bearing down on the island as if to swallow it whole, its large waves breaking into whitecaps.

❧

I still have a choice. I can stay on this bus. I can choose to return to P— with the driver. To change buses there and head to Seogwipo.

Phew, what foul weather . . . the driver mutters to himself as he returns to the bus, brushing the snow off his hair.

Settling back in his seat, he fastens his seat belt and starts the engine. He switches on the headlights and drives the bus into the storm at a slow crawl. The single-lane road winds through the dense forest of cryptomeria. Thousands of tall trees lurch in the gloaming under scattering snow. As if the black trees of my old dream were alive still, and this was their landscape.

5

Remaining Light

Snow falls.

On my forehead and cheeks.
On my upper lip, the groove above it.

It is not cold.
It is only as heavy as feathers,
as the finest tip of a paintbrush.

Has my skin frozen over?
Is my face covered in snow as it would be if I were
dead?

But my eyelids must not have grown cold. Only the
snowflakes clinging to them are. They melt into cold
droplets of water and seep into my eyes.

My jaw chatters. My teeth knock together. I'm afraid I'll bite my own tongue. Forcing my wet eyelids open, I find darkness. The same darkness I saw when my eyes were closed. Invisible snow-flakes fall into my eyes, and I blink.

With my hood still on, I turn my head and roll on to my side. I cross my arms tight and bring my knees up. I try gently moving my joints, from my neck down to my feet. I don't seem to have broken any bones. My thighs and shoulders ache, but the pain is not unbearable.

⁓

I have to get up and move. I can't afford to lose any more body heat. But I can't bring myself to do it. I don't know where I am. I don't know where I need to go.

I have no idea when my phone slipped out of my hand. As the grey-blue twilight vanished, I'd come to the first forked road and turned on the torch on my phone. With not much battery left, I had planned to use it only when I had an import-ant choice to make, like right then. I clearly remembered the path to Inseon's house as one that split off into two trails and was confused by the faint outlines before me, of three footpaths of different widths running through the woods. I thought the torch would allow me to recognize the route to take, but the white trees spilled their shadows at once at my phone's faint light, which only made the place that much more unfamiliar. Still, I had no time to hesitate. Relying on my memory of having gone down a wide trail with a gentle slope rather than the relatively narrow uphill one, I moved towards the widest of the three tracks. The very next moment, the ground gave beneath me as I fell through a heap of snow.

I'd instinctively covered my head with both arms. That must have been when I dropped my phone. As I tumbled down an incline, my head and body were pummelled by stones and rocks, but I didn't black out. My puffer coat, which was like a sleeping bag, and the snowdrifts on the way down helped to lessen the shock.

⌣

Had it become this dark in that short amount of time?

Had I lost consciousness after all, when I was so sure I hadn't?

I push up the sleeve of my coat with my trembling left hand. I feel around for my watch, knowing very well it doesn't light up in the dark. I see only blackness.

I realize my migraine, which had felt like having my eyes gouged out with a dull knife, is gone. Perhaps the shock has released my body's natural pain relievers or raised my heart rate. But the harsher cold remains. My teeth won't stop knocking together. My jaw throbs so much I worry it's about to come loose. The chill burrows its way into my cotton-filled hood and past my scarf. I hug my shivering knees as tightly as I can and think.

This path I've landed on and slipped down by accident, this bed of earth in which I am lying, is most likely the dried-up stream. A thin layer of ice must have set over its channel, a pile of snow heaped up over that. There are hardly any rivers or creeks on this volcanic island, and only occasionally during heavy rains or heavy snow do flowing streams appear. The village used to be divided along the border of this ephemeral stream, Inseon once told me on a walk. A cluster of forty houses, give or take, had stood on the other side, and when the evacuation orders went out in 1948, they were all set on fire, the people in them slaughtered, the village incinerated.

Until then, our house wasn't so far out of the way. Right across the stream, there used to be a village.

If I am indeed lying in that stream bed, then at least I didn't get turned around. If I can double back to the fork in the road, I'll be able to find my way. The problem is that I have no idea how far I've fallen. It may have been three or four metres, or more than ten. If only it weren't so murky, I would be able to tell which way to go. If only I had a lighter or a matchbook in my pocket.

⌒

I shouldn't have got off that bus.

Its chained wheels had left tracks in the snow as it slowly drove off, but by the time the bus disappeared back into the storm, huge snowflakes had already covered the tracks, erasing any trace of them.

Dim as it was, the snow reflected a greyish glimmer that lingered in the air, by which I could still make out things around me. The lights were off in the village's only shop, but a faint glow like that of a bedside lamp seeped out from underneath the door. I tried opening the sliding door just in case, but it was locked. Knocking, I got no indication that anyone was there. It didn't seem like a shop attached to a home.

Relying on the remaining light, I orientated myself and started walking. I veered away from the main road and crossed through the fields on paths lined by snow-capped basalt walls. I passed pitch-dark greenhouses and came to a road that ran through a small wood of conifers. Here, where the road was just barely wide enough for a small car to pass through, the snow came up to my knees. I had to plunge my legs in, then pull them back up to walk through the snowdrifts, which took time. My trainers and socks were drenched. Snow got in and on to my ankles and shins. There were no buildings I could use as landmarks, and as the trees around me were increasingly sunk in nightfall and half smothered with snow, I couldn't tell exactly what they were – all I could rely on was my sense of uphill and downhill, my memory of the road narrowing and widening.

My one relief as I traversed the woods was that the wind had eased up. The storm that had seethed so relentlessly against my face that I could barely open my eyes slowly subsided, and was almost at a lull. I moved forward, the sound of my legs trampling in and out of the snow the only thing to shatter the hush of the evening. I was afraid out there on my own, but it would have been worse if anything did appear at that moment — be it a wild animal or another person.

Judging from the heights and silhouettes of the trees, I seemed to be moving through a grove of cryptomeria. Last autumn, when I left Inseon alone with her woodworking to go on my walks to the bus stop, on my way back up I would see these tall trees swaying in the wind, rustling like fabric. It felt to me as though the wind on this island was always layered beneath everything else, an undertone. I felt its presence whether it was raging or gently ruffling the trees as it went by, and even on the rare occasions it was silent. Especially in the areas where the conifers and subtropical broadleaf trees grew together, the wind created an indescribable harmony as it passed through the branches and leaves, its speed and rhythm varying by the type of tree. Sunlight reflected off the lustrous camellia leaves, whose angles shifted from moment to moment. Vines of maple-leaf mountain yam wound around the cryptomeria trunks and climbed them to distant heights, swaying like swing ropes. Warbling white-eyes hidden somewhere out of sight trilled to one another as if exchanging signals.

On that snowy path, in the darkness that grew heavier by the second, I was once again reminded of that wind. With each step I took, I felt it, like a shadow that could take shape and manifest at any moment, an ink stain smeared on the reverse side of the stillness. Heavy snow fell endlessly in the twilight, and by the time the fork in the road appeared before me at last, the sky was obscured. I turned on the torch on my phone to see more clearly, and the snow-shrouded trees beamed back a chilling white light. Beneath the relentless snow, three paths engulfed in black ran outwards from the fork. When I looked back, the lone path that bore my deep footprints lay in silence.

I wonder about the bird.

Inseon had told me that to save her I had to get her water within the day.

But when does the day end for a bird?

These little ones fall asleep like a light going out.

That was how Inseon described it one evening last autumn, after she had let the birds out for an hour to fly around and then returned them one after the other to their cage. Before she draped a blackout cloth over them, she briefly looked the birds in the eyes.

They'll be wide-eyed and chirping like this, but as soon as the light's gone, they'll fall straight asleep. It's like they're hooked up to a power source. Even in the dead of night, if I pull this cloth away, they wake right up and start chirping and chattering again.

My coat doesn't reach my calves and feet, but they no longer feel cold. I touch my numb ankles with my gloved hands. I draw my knees closer. Now I'm curled into a ball, and I try huddling even deeper into myself so my coat can wrap around me and keep the wind from getting to my chest and stomach. But it's impossible to cover my feet.

Maybe I should be moving my toes more to counteract the numbness. I don't know whether frostbite has already set in. I remembered that the subject of the second short film in the series Inseon called a triptych – the woman who, at sixteen, had spent five days traversing the plains of Manchuria alone to find her way back to where an independence militia had set up camp – had lost four of her toes to frostbite along the way. Inseon inserted an interview after the scene she had filmed as she herself walked that same terrain, a small camera strapped to her forehead, the skies blue even as the dry snow whirled in the blustery weather.

It beats me, says an unseen narrator, how she managed to survive in that snow.

The voice of the woman's eldest daughter, who had agreed to be interviewed on behalf of her mother, overlays the whooshing wind and the crunch of footsteps.

My mum always told me it's warmer inside snow. She would dig a hole in the snow and wait in it until morning. Pinching herself to stay awake, so she wouldn't freeze to death.

The scene changes to a shot of the older woman, though I couldn't tell whether or not she was grasping what her daughter was saying. She sits in her wheelchair, wearing a cardigan the colour of rice with mother-of-pearl buttons, and stares absently at the sunlight outside the window.

She used to work at a textile factory in Pyongyang, the daughter continues, but when she heard, somewhat belatedly, that the night-school teachers she looked up to had joined an independence group, she sought them out. Her teachers were surprised to see her. What's a sweet little girl like you doing here? they asked. I think my mother might have had romantic feelings for one of the teachers, or at least admired him. She says she followed him into a transportation unit and went to work smuggling weapons and ammunition. She hid them in bundles wrapped in cloth and sneaked them on to trains, stashed them in sacks of grain and transferred them by truck. One day, she was staying at lodgings by a river with four others in her unit when Japanese soldiers raided the place, most likely after a tip-off. She heard the soldiers open and search the rooms one by one and, with the members who had been sharing the inner room, she'd escaped through the window. They took off running and leaped together into the pitch-black river. My mother told me she never understood how she alone managed to avoid the shower of bullets. She swam across and found herself unaccompanied on the bank. She told me the desire to know the reason she had been the only one spared was like a roaring flame inside her, and this was what kept her from freezing to death. Her river-drenched shoes never dried out and four of her toes fell off as she trekked back, though she wouldn't realize this until later, and when she did, she felt neither regret nor sorrow.

I've huddled my entire body barring my feet into my puffer coat and buried most of my face deep inside the hood, but there's nothing I can do to stop the snow from falling on the blade of my nose, my right eyelid. If I move a hand to wipe the snow away, the ball I've curled into will unfurl and, more importantly, the body heat I've generated will be lost, so I leave the gathering snow be. My jaw throbs as if it might fall out from the incessant chattering, and I bear the pain by biting down on my stiff snow-covered sleeve to still my teeth. A thought comes to me. Doesn't water circulate endlessly and never disappear? If that's true, then the snowflakes Inseon grew up seeing could be the same ones falling on my face at this moment. I am reminded of the people Inseon's mother described, the ones in the schoolyard, and release my arms from around my knees. I wipe the snow from my numbed nose and eyelid. Who's to say the snow dusting my hands now isn't the same snow that had gathered on their faces?

~

How does one endure it?
  Without a fire raging in one's chest.
  Without a you to return to and embrace.

~

Want some noodles? Inseon asked, and I remember the bird sitting on her shoulder clearly answering, Sure.

Inseon went to the fridge and took out a pack of wheat noodles from inside the door. Ama flew up from the table to sit on Inseon's other shoulder. Inseon pulled out a noodle, snapped it in half and held out a piece to each bird. She divided her attention evenly between them, watching one bird and then the other as they pecked at their food.

Want to try? she asked me.

Caught off guard, I accepted the pack of noodles from Inseon, and the birds immediately flew over to my shoulders. I snapped a stick of noodle and offered each half to the birds as Inseon had done, and then felt flustered as I wasn't sure which way to turn my head first. Each time the birds bit off a piece of the noodle with their beaks, I felt the faint impact on my fingertips, like the lead of a mechanical pencil as it breaks.

～

I don't know how birds sleep and die.

Whether their breaths are snuffed out when what remaining light vanishes.

Or whether their lives go on flowing, like electricity, into the early hours of dawn.

～

How long before it gets bright out?

The biting cold that had me shivering uncontrollably begins to relent. The temperature of the air almost certainly isn't rising, but I am suddenly overcome with sleep as though a mass of warm air is blanketing my coat. I hardly feel the chill of the snow landing on my eyelids.

Each time I nod off and let go of my knees, I jolt awake again and clasp my hands. I'm oblivious to the snowflakes falling on my face. I am no longer aware of their delicate brush-like touch nor of the droplets seeping into my eyes.

As warmth radiates through my body like bright ripples across water, I sink back into my dreamy, muddled thoughts. Don't the wind and the currents circulate too, not only water? The snow that fell over this island and also in other ancient, faraway places could all have condensed together inside those clouds. When, at five years old, I reached out to touch my first snow in G——, and when, at thirty, I was caught in a sudden rain shower that left me drenched as I biked along the riverside in Seoul, when the snow obscured the faces of the hundreds of children, women and elders on the schoolyard here on Jeju seventy years ago, when muddy water flooded the chicken coop as hens and baby chicks flapped their wings and rain ricocheted off the gleaming brass pump – who's to say those raindrops and crumbling snow crystals and thin layers of bloodied ice are not one and the same, that the snow settling over me now isn't that very water?

⁓

Thirty thousand people.

Inseon sits with her knees drawn up and her back against the sunlit wall. Instead of her face, the camera is trained on one shoulder and knee, so that most of the screen is taken up by the pale backdrop. A mysterious shadow ripples against the whitewash. Overgrown grass sways around her, brushing against the thin cotton-hemp blend of her shirt.

There were around thirty thousand murdered in Taiwan too, and one hundred and twenty thousand in Okinawa.

Inseon's voice is as calm as ever.

Sometimes I think about those numbers. And how these places are all islands. Isolated.

The light dancing on the wall expands until

the screen becomes a flat, beaming surface, capturing nothing.

～

Each time I am lured into sleep like I'm being pulled towards a warm light, I force my eyes open with my hands. I can't tell if it's drowsiness or the thin layer of ice over my lashes that is keeping them sealed.

Faces appear to me in my fading consciousness. Not the faces of dead strangers but of people who are living, albeit far away on the mainland. They are exhilaratingly clear. Vivid memories play out before me. In no particular order, and without context. Like a thousand dancers spilling on to the stage at once to each perform a different movement. Their bodies, suspended in their poses, shimmer like crystals.

I don't know if this is what happens right before you die. Everything I have ever experienced is made crystalline. Nothing hurts any more. Hundreds upon thousands of moments glitter in unison, like snowflakes whose elaborate shapes are in full view. How this is possible, I can't say. My every pain and joy, all my deep-rooted sorrows and loves, shine, not as an amalgam but as a whole comprised of distinct singularities, glowing together as one giant nebula.

⌒

I want to sleep.

I want to rest inside this euphoria.

I truly believe I will finally be able to drift off.

⌒

But there's the bird.

I feel something touch the pads of my fingers.

A delicate tapping, like a very faint pulse.

A trace wave of electricity trickling through my fingertips.

⌒

When had the wind started blowing again?

My body is no longer curled up like a ball. My fingers have unclasped. I raise a sluggish hand to my face to wipe away the ice from around my eyes. I hear the fierce winds tussling with the trees. Is that what woke me? I prise my eyes open. I'm stunned to find light. It's a faint light, a midnight blue just barely discernible from the darkness falling over the snowdrift beside my head.

Has the day already dawned?

Or am I dreaming?

No, this is no dream. A terrifying chill swoops down on me as if it's been waiting to strike. I lie back as neatly as I can as the shivering overtakes me, and look up at the sky. I can't believe it. The surrounding blackness is no longer absolute. It's stopped snowing too. The pale swirling in the air is the wind stirring up old snow. Revealed under the moonlight. For the winds have scattered the snow clouds and a pale half-moon now hangs over the woods. Massive storm clouds advance on heavy winds.

⌣

A faint bluish glimmer emanates from the dry stream winding its way up through the woods like a long white snake. I take one step at a time, leaning forward so I won't fall back. The moon appears and is obscured repeatedly by the charging clouds. All the treetops are swaying in its wan light, emitting a deep blue hue as if they'll never darken again. But beneath the canopy everything is murky and I can't tell one thing apart from another. I don't know what might be lurking inside that shadow, its gaping maw like that of a remote cave. Perhaps the dark stumps of thousands of trees. Perhaps birds and roe deer, not one making a sound.

At last, I spot the forked road. There is no trace now of where I fell, nor the trail I left as I plummeted downwards. The snow has blanketed everything. Pawing through the banks like a four-legged animal, I clamber up to the path. I can't locate the unusually deep hole where I'd lost my footing. If I were to comb the area, I might still be able to find my phone, but there's no time. The weather might shift again at any moment.

This time, I don't make a mistake. I head down the gentle slope for a bit, then follow the road as it levels out, relying on the light of the moon reflecting off the untrodden snow. The rustling and creaking of the woodland, the sound of my legs plunging into knee-high snow, the rasp of my breath, all commingling into one.

⌣

The faint pulsing in my fingertips slowly grows more pronounced.

The lingering feeling in my palm too, which I had forgotten about, returns and grows more vivid as if my blood is circulating anew.

When I absently caressed the white back of Ama's neck as she perched on my shoulder, the bird would stoop lower, then hold still, as if she was waiting for something.

She wants you to pet her more.

Obediently, I stroked the bird's warm nape again. She bowed even lower, as if in greeting, and Inseon laughed.

More. She's asking you to keep going.

⌣

I come to another fork in the road. As I step between the trees on to a narrow trail hidden under snow, a tangle of underbrush scratches my face. My skin must be frozen as I hardly feel any pain, but I narrowly missed getting poked in the eyes.

Have I made another misstep? Is there woodland beyond this point rather than a road?

I wipe my eyes with gloved hands, sensing a strangely wavering light. When I take off my gloves and rub my eyes again, my bare hands come away smeared in wet blood. But the blood isn't the problem. And I wasn't mistaken about the wavering light. Amid the threshing branches and the brushwood scattering snow, there's a faint bright spot. Pushing aside the underbrush with one hand and covering my face with the other, I press on.

There is something out there. Something luminous.

Once I come out on the other side of the brush, a long stretch of dark blue road appears. As it winds around the woods, the path brightens, until I see a radiant pool of silver at the end. I muster all my strength to pick up speed. Breathing hard, I forge ahead as best I can through the snow. When I reach the bend, I rub my eyes again and look directly at the light.

Inseon's workshop.

The iron door gapes open, revealing an island

of light inside. Did someone else get here before me? I shudder. Then it hits me.

No one's been by since that day.

When I didn't come to the door, though the light was on in my workshop, they stepped inside to check if everything was okay and found me lying there, unconscious.

While they rushed to load the bleeding victim on to the bed of their truck, no one had bothered to turn off the lights. There hadn't even been time to shut the door.

It stands wide open, as if expecting someone now. Wind gusts into the workshop, sucked inside along with the lustrous snow.

6

Trees

Stepping inside, I'm struck by the sight of huge logs, about thirty-odd of them, leaning against all four walls of the room. These are taller than the average person. Most are well over two metres and the few that are roughly my height would correspond to children aged twelve or thirteen.

There are logs lying in stacks on the floor. I step between them. On the cement, beneath the dusting of snow carried in on the wind, I notice splotches of blood. By the workbench, under more snow, a pool of blood has hardened to ice. That must have been where Inseon lay unconscious after injuring her fingers. A partially cut log, an unplugged angle grinder, ear protectors and various pieces of wood mottled by darkened blood lie on the workbench.

Neat rows of timber – Douglas fir, crypto-meria, walnut – usually fill this space. Along with fresh sawdust heaped around the bench like fine castella-cake crumbs, and an assortment of carpenter's tools sitting or hanging on shelves and walls. Inseon liked to keep this space clean and tidy. At six o'clock, towards the end of her workday, she would use the blow-gun attachment on her air compressor to remove flecks of wood from her hair. Next, she opened the front door and turned on a large air circulator to blast dust out into the woods. Woodchips she swept up and threw into a burlap sack, and heavier bits of wood the wind hadn't managed to stir were sucked up with a dust collector.

Whatever she might be working on, she made sure never to rush. On humid days, the room filled with the mingled scent of the various types of wood, and she said she took that as her cue to put the kettle on and make tea throughout the day. Because humidity makes wood heavier and increases its density, it was important to slow down to prevent any mishaps, she said. By adjusting her pace to the fluctuations in her work environment, Inseon managed nearly every aspect of her work on her own. Including oiling large pieces of furniture like chests of drawers, which required her to turn them over several times. She insisted that as long as she worked at her pace, used the tricks of the trade and gave herself plenty of time, she didn't need assistance.

This project, though – surely the scope of it would have been impossible to manage on her own. I had told her that the trees in my dream were as tall as people. Why then had she decided to scale them up?

⁓

I return to the entrance and close the door. I bolt the latch so the wind won't blow it open.

Taking care not to step on any blood or logs, I walk across the space. Nearing the back door, which opens on to the inner yard, I notice there are logs lined up by the wall that have been painted black. Inseon must have daubed them to gauge the effect. Seeing the gradations of black on bark, I get the sense that these trees are speaking. I'd imagined that smearing pine-soot ink over them would be like cloaking them in deep slumber, so why then do they now resemble people enduring a nightmare? The other logs are immersed in stillness – not a single expression, not the slightest tremor – and it's only these painted trunks that appear to be suppressing their inner turmoil.

I pause, unable to look away. But I can't afford to dawdle. Turning the doorknob, I push on the back door, but it doesn't budge. I pull. Nothing. I thrust the full weight of my body against it. A sliver of an opening appears at the top. Pressing my leg into the lower half of the door, I push again. I feel the door shove through the snowdrift on the other side to open a hand-span. Releasing my weight, I stop and reach through the gap with one hand to clear the snow away. I repeat this until I am able to squeeze myself sideways through the opening.

I leave the door open to light my way to the house. I plough through the bank of snow that is as high as my thighs, but after only a few steps I freeze in astonishment. There's a figure in the middle of the yard waving its long, black arms at me. I quickly realize that it's only a tree, but the frisson of shock remains.

In fact, it's the very same tree that crept up on me last autumn, some type of palm with fronds that droop like the branches of a weeping willow.

I thought someone was standing there! I'd grumbled from the central room of the house, from where I had a full view of the tree. Inseon chuckled.

It's even worse in the middle of the night, she said. I still startle. Wondering who it could be at that hour.

It was nightfall, not dawn, when we had that conversation. In the gentle breeze that embraced the dim twilight, the tree, which was a bit taller and wider than the average adult, appeared to be walking towards us, loose sleeves swishing at its sides.

Those same sleeves are whipping about more briskly than before in the strong gale. The tree looks set to rear itself up from the snow and amble towards me. I turn away. Pushing through the snow, I head for the darkened house.

~

In this murky gloom, Ama is probably asleep. I know she's unlikely to wake up and make her sharp chirp until I turn on a light, as I've seen her do in the mornings once Inseon has removed the cover from their cage.

That's what budgies sound like? I asked once.

Inseon laughed and said, I'm not sure, but that's how Ama and Ami cry.

They sound like white-eyes, I said.

Inseon laughed again. Who knows? Maybe they picked it up from a bird calling outside. I'm just glad it wasn't a crow, she added humorously.

⌐

I enter the house through the unlocked front door. Standing in the entryway, I remove my woollen gloves and stash them in the pocket of my puffer coat before pulling my soggy trainers and socks off my numbed feet. I slide the inner door open, step up on to the wooden floor and feel along the wall. I find the light switch and flick it on.

A faint wailing of wind seeps through the rafters, the windows and the doors, accentuating the lifelessness inside. The wide window facing the dark yard reflects my whole body back to me. Lowering the hood of my coat, I see my bloodied face and wild hair.

By this window, Inseon has placed a table she made from cryptomeria. The birdcage sits on it. The blackout cover and a few cleaning tools hang neatly from the metal hooks she's attached along one side of the table. The cage has one fixed perch and two matching swings, all made from bamboo that Inseon cut and sanded down and positioned at equal height to prevent a struggle for dominance between the birds.

In the thunderous stillness, which is as chilling as any sudden loud eruption, I walk towards the cage and its unoccupied perch and swings. The water dish is dry. The wooden dish Inseon fills with dried fruit and the square silicone container for pellets both stand empty. A handful or two of chaff is all that remains, strewn over a ceramic plate. And beside all this lies Ama.

⌣

Ama.

My voice echoes brokenly in the silence.

I've got you.

I lift the latch on the cage door with my cold-numbed fingers. I reach for Ama's head.

Come on now.
  I'm here to save you.

⌣

My fingers touch softness.

A softness without warmth.

A softness without life.

Nothing makes a sound.

Apart from my own breathing, and my trembling coat sleeve as it brushes against the wire mesh.

⌐

I stumble backwards into the kitchen. I open the cabinets, starting with the ones below the sink and moving on to the wall cabinets. Standing on tiptoe, I reach for a biscuit tin on the highest shelf. The tin is packed with teabags. I remove the lot and stack them on a shelf, then carry the tin to Inseon's room.

I open the door and switch the light on. A single mattress, a ninety-centimetre-wide wardrobe, a five-drawer chest, a desk, a monitor for video editing draped in a white cloth and bookshelves made from Douglas fir fill the room. The top shelf of the iron bookcase by the door is lined with sourcebooks flagged with sticky tabs, and paper storage boxes of all sizes are neatly packed into the remaining four shelves. I walk past the

boxes and the sticky notes that mark the dates
and details of their contents. I open the wardrobe
to find Inseon's usual five or six items of winter
clothing hanging to one side – otherwise the
space is mostly taken up by cameras and other
film equipment. Closing the wardrobe, I set to
opening drawers. The top drawer contains knick-
ers and socks; the second, summer as well as
spring and autumn clothes. In the third drawer, I
find a basket holding scarves and handkerchiefs.
I pick out a white handkerchief that looks barely
used. It is embroidered at one corner with small
violets.

⁓

I return to the birdcage.

A charged hush surrounds the small body, as if it
had been pulsing with blood mere moments ago.
As I look down, I get the sense that this severed
life is pecking at my chest, trying to tear its way
in. I feel its desire to burrow inside my heart, to
dwell there for as long as that organ goes on
beating.

As I wrap the bird in the embroidered

handkerchief, I can feel its cold delicate body through the thin material of the fabric. I gently tuck in the bird's half-open wings, fold the handkerchief once more over its body, then lay it in the tin. I've gathered the fabric around the bird as best I can, but the upper seam falls open and exposes the bird's face.

I return to Inseon's room. I look in the remaining drawers but don't find a sewing case. I walk over to the larger bedroom that was once her mother's room and turn on the light. The room exudes chill: it has obviously not been heated in quite a while. As usual, there's a cotton mattress spread out on the floor before the wardrobe, a cotton duvet neatly folded over it.

As I step on the thin floor mattress to reach the wardrobe, I remember the coping saw. I wonder if it's still there. Can saw blades ward off nightmares? Do dreams keep well away from their serrated edges?

I pull the old wardrobe doors open. Some of the mother-of-pearl inlays have become lost to time. Inside, past the faint scent of worn cloth and mothballs, I spot what could be a sewing case: a round metal tin wrapped in red silk, its exterior frayed and darkened from decades of use. I bend down and reach past the shabby cardigans and blouses hugging the gloom. I get the round tin out and open its lid. Inside I find several needles threaded with fine strands of white and black, a crude-looking thimble, assorted buttons, a rusty pair of sewing scissors and white sewing cotton wound round a makeshift spool, which is simply a thick piece of kraft paper folded lengthwise.

⌒

I gather and tuck the loosened cloth, cover the bird's exposed face. I wind a length of cotton thread round the handkerchief to secure it and snip the end with the sewing scissors. As I set about tying a knot, I rub my eyes to see what I'm doing and realize something's oozing from my eyes. I carelessly wipe my hand, now covered in the sticky discharge as well as blood from my earlier run-in with the bush in the woods, on the front of my coat. Stinging viscous tears well up again and gum up the wound. I don't know why. Ama wasn't my bird. I didn't care enough let alone love her to be feeling such grief.

The biscuit tin is only as wide as the span of my hand, but I'll need additional filler to prevent Ama's tiny body from being jostled or bruised. I loosen my woollen scarf and tuck it into the box, pressing into the corners. Being too narrow as well as too short, the scarf never quite kept my neck warm, but it fits snugly around the bird.

As I close the aluminium lid, it occurs to me that I should wrap the box in something to keep the vermin out. I find a clean white towel in a bamboo basket by the bathroom. I wrap the tin in it, then cut off a long piece of cotton thread and wind it twice round the towel before knotting the ends into a bow.

⌣

The snow is like a few dozen sacks of spilled sugar in the light pouring out of the house. I notice a broom made of twigs poking out from the drift below the eaves and fetch it. Holding the wrapped tin box in the crook of one arm, I start sweeping and find a wet shovel lying on the ground beneath the snow.

Where should I bury her?

I leave the tin under the eaves and pick up the shovel.

Where would Inseon bury her?

Feeling the cold wrap its fingers around my bare neck, I pull the hood of my coat over my head. I bend down and begin digging my way to the tree. Its trailing fronds are long black sleeves thrashing in the air. Midway through, I straighten and look behind me. The path I've burrowed resembles a narrow tunnel that leads to the tin box beneath the eaves.

Finally, I reach the tree. I shovel away the snow piled at its foot. As my breathing grows laboured, the cold recedes. Walking back to the front of the house to retrieve the tin, I notice that the pounding in my chest feels uncannily strong.

I lay the box down by the tree. I force the shovel into the earth I've uncovered. Placing my right foot on its head, I plunge the blade in with the weight of my body. The ground won't give. I step up with both feet and briefly totter as I find my balance, then feel the ground yield slightly. I repeat the movement, stepping up and down. Bit by bit, the metal sinks into the frozen earth. My arms and legs start to spasm. I know, of course.

That I should really get some warm food in me. That I should run a hot bath and try to sleep. But I can't – not until I've buried this bird.

At last, I feel the blade reach soft soil. Leaving the shovel rammed in the ground, I step down and look up at the sky as I catch my breath. The moon is gone. As are the murky clouds that had been advancing in its bright glow.

Is another snowstorm on its way?

I need to hurry.

I begin digging a hole for the tin. Then I feel something slick and cold graze my face. I startle, then shudder. It's the sleeve of a trailing frond. I lift my face. I feel flakes of snow brush my brows. In the light from the house, I can see a light flurry of fresh snow settling over the yard.

I wonder if it's snowing in Seoul. Sprinkling, with ice particles as fine as rice powder. Like the snow Inseon and I saw outside the noodle-shop window all those years ago. I picture commuters rippling out of a subway exit late at night, pulling their hoods over their heads as they walk into the snow. A handful opening the umbrellas they'd thought to bring. I picture tail lights glowing as vehicles wait for the green light, motorbikes zooming their way through the traffic and the weather. It doesn't seem quite right to know that Inseon is there and I'm not, that I'm here and she's not.

If there's a universe in which Inseon's fingers remain intact, in that same universe I would be curled up in bed still or I'd be sitting at my desk in my flat. Inseon would be asleep on her single mattress or working in the kitchen. Ama's toes would be curled round her perch. Her slumbering body warm in the darkness of the covered cage. Her heart beating steadily beneath the down of her chest.

When did it stop beating? If I hadn't fallen into the dry stream, could I have brought her water before her heart stopped? If I had chosen the right path in that split second and continued on my way? Or, going back further, if I had waited at the terminal for the bus that would take me over the mountain?

∼

I dust off the snow that has settled on the tin and set it down in the hole. The box won't sit flat. I rake and smooth the black earth at the bottom of the pit with my hands, then wipe the snow from the tin again. I crouch on my heels for a moment as if I'm waiting for a signal that won't come before placing the box inside. Using my hands again, I scoop dirt over the tin until I can't see its pale surface any more. I continue with the shovel, throwing the soil I've dug back into the hole in a heap, after which I pack it down firmly with the palms of my hands into a small mound. Then I sit back and watch its black surface disappear beneath the cover of snow.

⌣

There's nothing more to do.

In a few hours, Ama's body will have frozen. And will remain preserved until February, at which point it will rapidly decompose. Until it is a handful of feathers and perforated bones.

⌣

I shovel a path to the workshop to switch off the light and shut the back door. There's a large tarpaulin pulled over something outside the work-shop wall. I lift the tarp and find a big pile of logs. Their rough, raw bark is visible beneath the rubber cords that bind them together to keep them from toppling.

With the logs inside that makes over a hundred in total.

Above them on the limewashed wall, a shadow flickers. A shadow cast by the tree beneath which I've just buried Ama, in the light from the house. I stare at its soundless lurching, the fronds like flailing arms. I recall that this wall served as the backdrop to Inseon's self-interview in her last film. The shadow agitating against the wall in sunlight was the same shadow I see now.

Inseon had worked on that film before she moved here, back when this shed was mainly used for storage. On the screen, only her shoulder, knee, and the pale line of her neck were visible, as though she herself were an intruder in a scene dominated by the shadow. The shadow heaved, creating a sense of foreboding. Waving arms protesting Inseon's testimony. Grasping hands thrust forward only to jerk back. Injecting a deliberate and persistent note of dissonance to the interview.

⌣

I went back a few times to look for that cave, but I never found it.

I searched my memory, tried to retrace my steps, but I failed.

No. I didn't dream it.

The winter I turned nine was the last time we were there.

The interview begins in medias res. The questions posed have been edited out, or perhaps there were none to begin with.

The caves on this island have narrow mouths. Barely wide enough for one person to squeeze through. Roll up a rock outside and they're impossible to find, but as you go deeper the caves open up. There's one cavern where folk from an entire village were able to hide out in the winter of '48.

A forest fills the screen. It seems to have been filmed with a head camera. Everywhere the camera's eye falls, large deciduous trees soar up, stirring in the wind. The tree canopy obstructs the light; nothing green grows on the forest floor, which is in partial shade. Fallen tree limbs bearing big leafage, roots articulated and jutting like the joints of giants, the soundless dappling over the earth of patterns cast by the odd ray that's broken through – and throughout, the constant sound of soil crumbling underfoot.

The cave my father and I used wasn't that big. At most ten people could have hidden there.

The screen returns to the limewashed wall. Inseon's hands are folded in her lap in the bright light. There's a moment when the air grows still and the shadow of a single frond, which had resembled an agitated sleeve, for a brief second assumes the distinct outline of a curled fern leaf.

I remember it being always damp, the air. It was always raining or snowing when we went in. I don't recall us ever heading to the cave on a clear day, so it could be that he was reacting to drops in air pressure. Like folk complaining of aching joints on wet, cloudy days.

Her voice drops to a whisper.

Shh, let's soksom now.
He always said this when we were in hiding.

The fern leaf rises up, gliding soundlessly over the wall.

Meaning, hush your breath. Don't move. Don't make a peep.

Her interlaced fingers loosen, then draw tighter together.

I remember the light coming in around the rock blocking the cave mouth. Father putting his thick jacket around me. Placing his palm against my forehead when I had no fever, then lowering his voice to say, Mind you don't catch cold now. Keep your wits about you and you won't get sick. Remember that.
When I whispered back to ask if we could go home, he said firmly, We shouldn't be at home now.

How are we to sleep in this cold? I asked, and he said something I didn't understand.

No such thing as night and day, he said. In military operations.

Umung will be waiting, though, I said.

I felt his body flinch and shudder at the word, felt it like a current that had leaped from him to me.

That's why she ought to have followed us, he said.

I remember how he looked before the little bit of light from outside grew faint, then dark. His eyes towards the little crack, a glossy sort of light in his eyes and on the sleet on his grey hair.

What could I do? I couldn't drag her here against her will. I had to save the child. The child's done naught wrong.

I didn't know what scenes were flashing in his mind then, but I understood that he clasped my hand every time he reached a despairing conclusion. I felt the soundless tremors that seeped from him and wet my hand like water wrung from dripping clothes.

A map of the island, its contour an oval stretched east to west, appears on the screen. Above graphics stating that the map is part of US military records from 1948, a conspicuously thick line demarcates the boundary five kilometres off the coastline. Hallasan and its immediate surrounding areas are to be evacuated and anyone seen passing there will be considered an insurgent and shot and killed without exception, announces the decree in subtitles. A succession of remarkably clear, noise-reduced and silent black-and-white shots follow. Scenes of thatched roofs burning. Plumes of black smoke rising amid fiery sparks. Soldiers in light-coloured uniforms with bayonet-fitted rifles slung on their shoulders, jumping over stone field walls.

The dark.

The dark is pretty much all I remember.

I kept drifting off and reopening my eyes in confu-sion. Later still, I'd jolt awake to remember I was in a cave, not at home, and to feel my father's hand still holding mine, even if his face and the rest of his body were invisible. I would have cried out if it weren't for that hand. I'd have called for my mother and wept. I think he knew this and that's why he held my hand. Maybe he sat in the dark, ready to clasp his other hand over my mouth. In case I made a noise as I slept. In case any creature passing out-side found us.

This is followed by archival footage of civilians being trucked past an oreum flush with silver-grass. It's filmed from behind, presumably from another vehicle chasing the truck. Two police-men stand guard at the front and rear of the cargo bed, where a few dozen people, including women, infants and elders, sit with their backs and shoul-ders touching. A child of about five with cropped hair presses her body into a young woman who looks to be her mother and stares at the camera until she is no longer in the frame.

If it started to snow as we walked to the cave, my father would snap off a cane of broadleaf bamboo.

We are back in the shaded forest, Inseon's camera moving at her slow pace.

He'd tell me to walk on ahead and he'd fall behind. Walking sideways like a crab, he swept over our trail with the bamboo cane to erase our footprints. Now which way do I go, Appa? I'd stop to ask and he would calmly direct me. Once we left the trails and went deeper into the hill, he carried me on his back to get us up the slope. He went on sweeping, but now he had only one set of footprints to hide. I clung to his back and watched the prints disappear. It was like magic. Like we were people who fell from the sky each second, the way we kept going and left no trace.

Three black-and-white photographs appear on the screen one by one, then fade away.

Four men in white clothes stand in a black pine forest. Four soldiers in tin hats are adjusting target vests over the men in white. Each of the four pairs of men are in close-up and the tender outline of each youth's nose, indented upper lip, chin and neck are clearly visible. One youth whose face is closest to the camera and so most prominent has clamped his lips tight in seeming fear, and beneath the thin skin of his neck his Adam's apple protrudes.

In the next photograph, the four young men are in target vests and each tied against a pine tree. The angle is wider and shows the soldiers assuming prone firing positions at no more than a five-metre distance.

The final photo shows the four youths, contorted. Upper bodies bulging forward above bound waists. Chins tipped, heads thrown back. Knees buckled. Mouths agape.

He was soft-spoken, my father.

Inseon's hands settle gently on her knee as she sits by the limewashed wall. She has a habit of placing her hands, palms down, in front of her when she is deep in thought. The shadow cast by the fronds has appeared as one overlapping shadow, but a wind stirs and the shadow becomes two, then three. Like hands groping along a wall, the shadows shift and alter their shape moment by moment.

My mother said to me once, If your abang had been manly, I wouldn't have taken to him. The first time I saw him, I thought how lovely his face was for a man. I guess fifteen years without sunlight left him as pale as a mushroom. I found it strange that folk avoided him. Like he'd come back from the dead. Like they might catch the ghost too if they so much as exchanged looks with him.

Inseon's knee and hands disappear from the screen, leaving only her voice. The shadows flick like whips over the wall, suddenly ferocious. Inseon's voice is almost a whisper.

On days when my father wasn't quite himself and sat and stared all day, my mother would call me. She'd grab whatever was to hand, a couple of raw sweet potatoes or cucumber slices, one or two mandarins, push them into my hands and say, Take these to your abang. If he won't eat them, you pop them in his mouth.

I guess she was hoping a bite of food would bring him out of his spell. And sometimes it did. He'd take the mandarin from me and try to smile. It was like he lived in two worlds. The room would be dark but he'd squint his eyes to look at me, as if he saw me with one eye but saw something else too with his other eye, a light that lay far beyond me.

~

I switch off the light in the workshop, close the door and turn away from the logs that reveal their rough-hewn cross sections with the flapping of the tarp. With the shovel tucked at my side, I retrace my steps. I get to the house, stamp my feet once I'm in the entryway and lock the door. Not that anyone would make their way here in the snow and the gloom.

As I sit on the inner doorsill to remove my shoes, I am overcome by vertigo and lean back until my upper body's flat on the floor. I leave my bare feet on my soggy trainers and close my eyes. White motes replay behind my eyelids like some hallucination, lines of snow going every which way as they've done all day, scattering and falling at multiple angles.

The wind wails in through the front door. The door judders at my feet, as if someone's pounding on it. A sour taste creeps up the base of my tongue. I carefully turn to one side and try to regulate my breathing. If I remain still, I might not be sick. If I keep still, taking deeper, slower breaths.

But I press my palms to the wooden floor and pick myself up. I rush to the kitchen and heave into the sink. All I bring up is clear liquid, as I haven't eaten all day. I need my meds. A single packet from the generous stash I keep in the desk drawer at home in Seoul, in the paper bag from the pharmacy. The doctor has warned that prolonged use will damage my heart, but it's the only medication that works for me.

⁓

My hand shakes as I place the kettle on the hob. I switch off the main light and leave only the dim lamp above the dining table on. Now I can see the snow thrashing outside the window. The wintry scene outside superimposes on the scene reflected in the glass: the flapping tarp and waving tree arms are overlaid on the wooden table, the empty birdcage.

I switch the heat off before the water boils and take slow sips of the hot liquid from a mug. Savouring its warm movement down my throat, I lie down on the floor by the sink. I straighten my back and start deepening my breath. Turning to one side to prevent retching.

With each long exhale, the pain recedes. With each inhale, it advances to gouge my eyes again. I slip in and out of consciousness. Every time I come to from the pain, I see a pale outline of bones. It's from a scene towards the end of Inseon's last film, a close-up long shot of a trench filled with the remains of hundreds of people.

The shot lasts about a minute. No context, no explanation is given. Skeletal remains curled up in the foetal position, waists draped in disintegrated clothing, small foot bones shod in rubber, all overlapping, lying one on top of another, in a trench not much bigger than a furrow.

⌒

I feel feverish. My body starts to shiver. Everything feels cold against my skin. The outer fabric of my coat sleeve grazing my wrist may as well be a blade of ice. I remove the coat. I loosen my watch and push it towards the wall. I creep to the bathroom and vomit clear fluid into the sink. I rinse my mouth and wash my hands with soap. My hands that wrapped and tucked the bird in cloth, that dug up soil and raked it smooth, that patted the earth into a mound. I splash warm water on my face and the open wound starts to bleed again. Leaning on the sink to hold myself up, I look at the bloodied face in the mirror.

It was cold.

No, it was soft.

It was as hard as rock, I murmur out loud, correcting myself.

Each time I speak, the blood-soaked face soundlessly parts its lips.

No, it was as light as cotton.

⌒

The front door rattles as though someone is there. The windows to the back of the house shake against their sills. Snow gusts over the furniture reflected in the back window. The tarp swells like an air balloon in between the ropes holding it down.

The lamp over the table shudders, goes black. An inky torrent descends and erases both the indoor and outdoor scenes. I reach out and grope the air as I fumble my way out of the kitchen to the central room. The wall is further away than I thought. I find the switch for the ceiling light and flick it on. Nothing.

The power's gone.

I've heard Inseon say that snowstorms here could cause power and water cuts. That she sometimes had to wait several days for the repair crew to drive up, and that the more remote homes like this one were the last to have their power restored.

I should probably store up some water before

it goes. I carefully manoeuvre my way back to the kitchen. I open the cabinet and feel about under the sink for the two pots I remember seeing down there. As I place them in the sink and on the counter, I hear something fall and break over the floor. It must be the mug from earlier.

I fill the pots with tap water. It occurs to me that since the boiler is out I won't have heating.

I cover my hot eyes with wet hands and focus on my breathing. I hunker down to wait until the dry heaves pass, then crawl to Inseon's room, sweeping fragments of broken ceramic aside as I go.

In the bottom drawer of the chest, I find Inseon's sweater. It is shapeless and faded. I couldn't say what colour it had been. I pull it on over my own sweater. I open the wardrobe and grab the first coat to hand. An old duffel, judging from the feel of its bobbly exterior and long toggle buttons. I button up the coat to my neck and lie down on Inseon's mattress. I pull the cotton duvet over my head and endure the chills. Each time the front door and windows clatter in the wind, I turn towards the night and remind myself I'd hear different sounds if someone were there. A visitor would knock. They'd call out to the owner of the house. They wouldn't pound the door or rattle it against its frame.

～

Each time I pass out, a sharp dream splinters in. I am walking over to the sink, the bird's body in my cupped hands. A thin layer of ice surrounds it. Under warm running water, its face instantly softens. I wait for its eyes to open. For their familiar gleam. To see its beak move. *You'll breathe again, won't you, Ama? Your heart will beat once more. Yes, and you'll drink again, won't you?*

As soon as one dream wanes, another jabs its way in, a menacing ice pick. Earth, now a glacial globe, turns on its axis with an ear-splitting screech. Continents covered in churning, cascading lava have instantly turned to ice. Thousands of birds flock over the suddenly eternally unapproachable surface. They fall asleep as they glide. Coming to, they flap their wings. Then slice through the air, glinting, like skate blades.

～

Shall we sing, Ama?

The words are barely out of my mouth and the bird is already humming. While Ama hums from her perch on my shoulder, I kneel and dig up the earth. I have no shovel, no hoe. I scratch at the hard ground with my fingers. I dig until my nails splinter and my fingers bleed. The humming stops abruptly and I lift my head. Wet flakes of snow flutter down in the surrounding blackness, as they did when I came to in the stream bed. They land on my forehead. And beneath my nose. And on my lips.

I startle awake with teeth chattering and recall that I'm not in the dry stream or the yard but in Inseon's room. I need that saw, I think to myself between dream and reality. If I'm to defeat all this. So all this will pass me by.

Enjoy your visit.

Inseon's mother's voice whispers in my ear. Her hands lie small and cold in my palms like two dead birds.

⌒

You have to keep an eye on them even when they look fine, Kyungha.

They'll remain upright until they fall off their perch, and by then it's too late.

The front door and windows rattle. Maybe it isn't the wind. Maybe someone's actually there. Maybe they've come to drag out whoever's inside. To slash and burn. To fit with target vests and tie up against trees. Against that black tree as it brandishes its saw-blade arms.

I've come to die, I think from the depths of my fever.

I've come here to die.

To be cut open, riddled with holes, strangled, burned.

To this house as it is about to breathe fire and collapse in on itself.

To lie alongside these felled logs, these heaped fragments of a giant's shattered body.

PART TWO

Night

I

We Do Not Part

The tide was going out.

The waves, which loomed like cliffs, did not swallow the coast but were instead dragged out to sea. A basalt desert ran out to the horizon. Volcanic cones emerged from underwater like massive burial mounds, soaked and glittering black. Tens of thousands of fish that had not been swept away with the tide flailed about on the seabed, scales shimmering. Scattered over the black bedrock were the white bones of what might have been sharks or whales, the remains of wrecked ships, gleaming rods of rebar, wood planks wrapped in tattered sails.

I could no longer see the ocean. Gazing out across the desert at the horizon, I realized the island was no longer an island.

I looked back. The slopes of the snow-capped

mountain ran out from the peak like the ribs of a fan. The trees were scorched black as if they had been set ablaze. Leafless and branchless, they stood like pillars of ash, mutely overlooking the dark wilds.

What happened here? I wondered, feeling a pressure inside my mouth, which for some reason would not open. Where are the branches, the leaves?

The awful answer was lurking behind my tongue.

They're dead.

I clenched my jaw to keep from saying it aloud. I bore the pain of a bird beating its way out of my throat.

They're all dead.

The words filled my mouth, beak open, talons stretched. I shook my head, refusing to spit out what felt like writhing tufts of cotton wool.

~

It falls.

Floats.

Showers.

Gusts.

Churns.

Storms.

Lashes.

Drifts.

Shrouds.

Erases everything.

I couldn't tell what made the nightmares leave. I wasn't sure whether I had fought them off or whether they had crushed me at last and moved on. I only knew that, at some point, all that remained behind my eyelids was the snow. Swirling, mounting, freezing.

I lay in the grey-blue light that seeped its way into my shut eyes. I blinked them open and saw the west-facing window. The muted light of a day too overcast to leave clear shadows filtered into the room. Inseon's long black coat hung on the wall, its shoulders seemingly drawn together in thought.

My fever had gone down. The headache and nausea had subsided too. All the muscles in my body were loose, as if I'd been injected with an anticonvulsant. The cuts under my eyes no longer stung.

Reaching out from where I lay on the mattress, I pressed my hand to the linoleum floor. It was ice cold. I exhaled a white cloud of breath and pushed myself up on to my feet. In one of Inseon's drawers, I found some woollen socks and put them on, then took her heavy coat off the wall and slipped it on over her duffel. This was the coat she had worn back in Seoul, the one she had hand-sewn an old, worn cardigan into. Black lint beaded the sleeves like drops of water. There were mandarin peels that hadn't entirely dried in the right-hand pocket. I buttoned the outer coat up to the neck, inhaling the faint scent of pine resin with each breath.

I stepped over the wooden threshold of the sliding door, which I hadn't closed all the way the previous night, and into the central room. Light was coming in through the window, and snow was falling outside. Great big flakes of it, like so many white birds descending soundlessly through the air.

⁓

The hands on the wall clock above the refrigerator pointed to four o'clock. Too bright outside to be dawn, I knew it had to be four in the afternoon.

I was thirsty.

I tried turning on the tap at the sink, but, as expected, no water came out. Luckily, the water in the pot I had filled up right after the power went out was clean. I brought the pot to my lips and took a sip, then another. I stood there for a moment, feeling the cold water spread through my body, then stooped down to pick up the broken mug.

I needed a broom and dustpan to collect the pieces that had scattered across the floor. Remembering that Inseon had a set she kept by the front door, I crossed the central room to get them. The first thing that caught my eye when I opened the door to the entryway, though, was the torch sitting atop the shoe cabinet. It felt quite heavy as I switched it on, but the beam was faint, maybe because there was too much surrounding brightness. I was sweeping the column of weak light back and forth across the dark wooden floor, wondering if the batteries had died, when my breath caught.

The sound of a bird, crying out.

The pale beam from the torch shone through the birdcage and revealed a bird on the perch inside. Again, it chirped.

Ama.

My voice broke and scattered in the stillness.

You were dead.

I moved towards the wire cage, the door to which I had left half open after taking the bird out the night before. The inside remained littered with grain husks. The water dish was still bone-dry. The short white tufts sprouting from Ama's chest and the crown of her head looked soft as cotton. Her long white feathers gleamed, lustrous. She cocked her head and studied me with tiny eyes that glistened like wet black beans.

I buried you, just last night.

Am I dreaming? I wondered out loud.

The cuts beneath my eyes began to sting again, as if on cue. A glacial chill seeped from the floorboards through the woollen socks on my feet. With each exhale, my breath steamed into the sharp, cold air. I turned to look out at the yard, the heavy snow. I had buried you beneath that tree, though its shape had been rendered unrecognizable by the armour of snow that amassed around it overnight.

It was impossible for the bird to have returned. To have wrestled her way out of the handkerchief I had wrapped and secured her in, to have unravelled the string I had twined and knotted tight round the fabric, to have opened the aluminium tin I had sealed shut over her, to have snapped the string I had cross-wound over the towel in which I had bundled that tin. To have burst through the snow heaped up on her frozen burial mound, and to have flown in through the locked door to alight on this perch inside her cage.

Ama chirped again. Still watching me with eyes like moistened beans.

Give Ama some water.

I walked towards the sink, obeying a voice – Inseon's voice – I couldn't actually hear. I ladled some water from the big pot and carried it over to the birdcage, letting the water slosh over the sides of the bowl with each step. Ama waited, not moving a muscle as I poured some out for her. Only when I stepped back did she flutter up and settle on the small perch by her water dish.

I watched Ama nip the water with her beak, look up to swallow, then repeat.

Were you thirsty? I asked.

She paused and turned her head to look at me.

Is there such a thing as feeling hungry when you're dead? I asked.

Just when I felt like I would never be able to decipher the expression in her beady eyes, Ama lowered her head again. She opened her beak, took another nip of water and raised her head to swallow.

I scanned the dark refrigerator with the torch. All Inseon had for herself to eat were some vegetables, soaked sticky rice and half a block of tofu sitting in water. There was a much greater variety of food for the bird, and everything had been stocked with care. Sealed glass bottles of different sizes, clear banchan containers and ziplock bags variously held multicoloured pellets, millet, raisins, dried cranberries, walnuts, sliced almonds. The wheat noodles she used to give as a snack sat in the door of the fridge. There was an opened pack with half the noodles left and two that remained unopened.

What was Ama's staple food, though? I didn't know whether to feed her a little of everything, or whether to mix a couple of things into a meal and feed her some of the others as a snack. I had taken out the millet, dried cranberries and walnuts when I heard noise coming from the birdcage. Ama had pushed the door all the way open with her beak and escaped. She flapped her wings and soared up, nearly hitting the ceiling, then traced a huge circle in the air before alighting on the dining table.

Inseon had told me that the birds had to eat their meals, if not their snacks, inside the cage. Otherwise they would get into the habit of not wanting to go inside, which meant you lost the means to get them to sleep on time, and then all routine went out of the window. But did a dead bird have to abide by the same rules?

I got a large ceramic plate from a shelf above the sink and poured out a handful of millet. I snipped the cranberries into smaller bits with a pair of kitchen scissors and sprinkled them next to the grains. The finely chopped walnuts went in the centre, the soy-sauce dish filled with water to one side.

Come eat, Ama, I called, setting the plate on the table.

Ama chirped as if to say something was wrong.

It's all right, I said. Come and eat.

The bird walked across the table towards the plate. She pecked at the millet first, then drank some water. A grain of millet, a sip of water, two grains, one sip, a piece of cranberry, two sips.

You were hungry, I said. The moment the words left my mouth, a wave of unbearable hunger came over me. I took a fistful of dried fruits from the ziplock bag and tossed them in my mouth, a surprising burst of sweetness spreading as I chewed. If not for the power outage, I thought, I would cook up something warm on the electric stove. I would make some rice juk. I would take out the tofu soaking in the bowl of water and fry it till it was nice and golden.

⁓

I poured myself a glass of water and fixed a small plate of uncooked tofu and walnuts to bring to the table, where I sat down across from the bird to eat. I swallowed a bite of the tofu, which was salty from the bittern, and asked the bird, How long do you think it'll snow?

Ama's bowed head was small and round, like a chestnut. Surely the back of her neck would be warm to the touch. She didn't seem dead in the slightest.

This isn't a dream, is it, Ama?

I looked at the snow coming down in neat, unwavering lines outside the window, filling the empty sky that was darkening by degrees. The tree under which I had buried Ama stood unmoving, clad in snow.

Is this a dream?

I held out my hand to Ama, who had stopped eating. She hopped easily into my palm. The moment her rough feet scraped my skin, the cold vanished, and my heart and eyes were at once set aflame.

⁓

I gently petted Ama's neck. Every time she lowered her head, asking for more rubs, I obliged her. She dipped her head lower and lower. I petted her until she stopped.

When Ama, seemingly tired of this game, flew off and went to sit on the window ledge, I looked over at her, still thinking about the slight weight and pressure on my palm from where her feet had dug in a moment earlier.

You'll get cold there, Ama, I said, from all the draught.

If there's such a thing as feeling cold when you're dead. Well, where there's hunger, there must be cold too, I figured. That was when I remembered the wood-burning stove in the workshop. If I could get a fire started, it would be warmer in there than it was in here. I could take the pot in there and make some juk too.

Wait here, Ama, I said, getting up from the table. I'll get a fire going.

Ama flew up from the ledge. She let out a

long cry and settled on the shaded lamp that hung above the table. I smiled at the sight of her perched atop the light, swinging with each sway of the pendant cord.

I'll be back for you soon, I said.

⌒

Not a trace remained of the footprints I had made going back and forth between the workshop and the main house. To get through the snow, I had to make a new path. I retrieved my shovel, which was buried up to the tip of its handle in snow, and was shaking it off when something made me pause. The largest snowflake I'd ever seen had landed on the back of my hand.

It didn't feel cold, not in that moment, not right away. In fact, it was barely touching my skin. Only when the finer points of the crystal began to blur into ice did I feel a subtle pressure, a softness. The mass of the ice slowly diminished. Its whiteness dissolved into a drop of liquid on my hand. As if my skin had absorbed all its light, leaving only the particles of water behind.

It looked unlike anything I had ever laid eyes on. There was nothing else in the world with such a delicate structure. Nothing this cold and light. Nothing that remained this soft, right until the moment it melted and was undone.

In a strange fit of passion, I closed my hand round a fistful of snow, then reopened it. The snow on my palm felt as light as the fluffy down of a bird. As my palm swelled a soft pink, the snow absorbed my heat and turned into the world's softest ice.

I'll never forget this, I thought. I won't ever forget this softness.

But it quickly grew too cold to bear and I brushed the snow off my hand. I wiped my wet palm on the front of the coat. Within seconds it had turned stiff. I rubbed it with my dry hand. The heat refused to spread. I felt a shivering in my chest, as if all the warmth in my body had leached out through my hand.

❦

As soon as I cleared away the snowdrift behind the workshop and wrenched the back door open, a long shaft of light from the yard entered the gloomy interior. I walked inside, my back to the brightness, and switched on the torch. I aimed it towards the stove and, taking care not to step in the blood on the floor, followed the path of its beam as it swayed with the movement of my arm. As I approached the shadow the unplugged power grinder was casting over the workbench, I stopped short, catching sight of what appeared to be the silhouette of a person.

The black, rounded form shuddered and grew long. The body was extending itself out of its huddled pose. Its knees straightened, its two feet touched the ground. Its face, which had been buried in its arms, turned towards me.

. . . Kyungha-ya.

A raspy voice, like that of someone just waking up, abraded the air.

I switched off the torch and hid it behind my back on instinct. I couldn't let her see the blood-stains on the floor. The pewter light coming in through the back door shone dimly on Inseon's face, and I could read her expression even with-out the torch.

When did you get here?

Her face was pale and gaunt, though not to the extent that it had been in the hospital. She was rubbing her eyes with her right hand, which looked immaculate, entirely unscathed.

How did you get here? You didn't even call ahead.

Inseon's eyes, which looked bigger in the dark, stared hard at my face.

How'd you hurt yourself?

Got scratched up by a tree.

Oh dear, she sighed, eyes dimming.

Then in a low voice, she asked, Why are the lights off? She murmured to herself almost as an afterthought, *I didn't turn them off.* Frown lines creased her forehead.

There's a power outage, I told her.

How do you know that? Inseon asked, but her eyes moved from my face towards the yard as if she didn't want to hear my answer.

When did we get all this snow? Her voice wasn't directed at me . . . *Is this a dream?*

She stood motionless, watching the snow. The flakes were like white birds that grow heavier as they descend. When she finally turned her gaze back towards me, I saw that her face had subtly changed. Her eyes glistened with soundless tears, as if all the warm affection she'd stored for me over the last twenty years was seeping out at once.

I hardly ever fall asleep in here — I don't know

what I was doing knocked out like that, she grumbled softly. She hugged herself and asked me, Aren't you cold?

Familiar laugh lines creased the skin around her eyes.

Should I get a fire going?

I watched without a word as Inseon opened the little door of the wood-burning stove and tossed in a few small pieces of firewood. Her work uniform was a pair of worn jeans and sturdy shoes with a starched navy apron over a grey turtleneck sweater. She wore a familiar black cotton parka over that, the buttons left undone and the sleeves rolled up so as not to get in her way, revealing her bony wrists. With her right hand – fingers intact, unstitched, unbloodied – she grabbed two fistfuls of sawdust from a pail and scattered it over the wood. Striking the head of a match on one side of a large eight-sided matchbox, she said, You can't even find these matches in Seoul now.

Her face, as she waited for the fire from the sawdust to catch on the wood, was composed yet bereft.

I bought these at the little shop down by the bus stop. That must have been a decade or two ago, but they still burn well.

Soon the flames inside the stove shot up, casting a warm glow over the mounds of her eyes and the ridge of her nose.

～

Inseon placed the lone three-legged stool she had beside the stove. Sit here, she said.

Where will you sit?

Instead of answering, she hoisted herself on to the workbench. She swung her legs slowly like a child, her feet almost but not quite touching the ground, seemingly unaware that the blade of the electric saw was covered in her own blood.

With my hands still behind my back, I approached the stool and sat down. While Inseon's gaze lingered on the stove, I stashed the torch underneath the chair. The tips of my toes touched the sawed end of a piece of log laid across the floor. A dark stain formed over the dried pool of blood beside the log as the snow that had drifted in on the wind melted over it.

I peered at the vents drilled into the side of the stove like a pair of eyes. The flames were dancing inside. As the wood caught fire and began to crackle, the room filled with the sound of splitting tree bark.

I thought about you a lot.

I looked up at Inseon's voice. She was also staring at the vent.

I thought about you so much that some days it felt like you were here with me.

The flames flickered silently in her eyes. Her demeanour — the fact that she did not ask anything else — was as calm and unwavering as ever, to the point where I almost felt sure that what I imagined she was thinking now might be true. That she had in fact been here all along woodworking as usual, that the message I had got from her in Seoul and everything I had experienced on this island were only the illusions of a dead soul.

That reminds me. There's something I wanted to show you.

Pointing to the logs leaned up against the wall, Inseon asked, How do they look?

I answered honestly. I'd imagined they would be as tall as people, I said.

I tried that too, at first.

I thought she would tell me the reason why she had changed the scale, but she didn't waste her breath. Climbing down from the workbench, she asked casually, How about some tea?

I watched her stride across the workshop, towards the door that opened out to the woods.

I suppose since there's no power, we could burn solid fuel in the main house . . . but the fumes aren't good for Ama, so let's have the tea here.

Inseon raised her voice as she grew further away from me. When she opened the front door, the room became much brighter. Using that light to rummage through the freezer compartment in the small fridge near the door, Inseon hummed a bar of a song I didn't know. Was she going to boil more sour, bland wild berries?

Scooping the contents of a container out and into the kettle with a wooden spoon, Inseon asked, What are we calling it? Our project.

She turned to me, smiling as she poured bottled water into the kettle. I realized I'd never asked, she said.

We Do Not Part, I answered.

Approaching me with the kettle and two mugs in her hands, Inseon echoed the words. *We Do Not Part*.

In the rush of air coming through the open rear and front doors, we could see the flames surge higher inside the vents. Inseon set the kettle on the stove, which was now bright red from the heat. With a sound like sand sifting, beads of water rolled off the kettle and instantly turned to steam.

We sat without speaking, without facing each other. Only when we heard the water at the bottom of the kettle start to boil did Inseon break the silence.

As in we refuse to part by refusing to say goodbye, or as in we actually don't part ways?

There was still no steam coming out of the kettle. We had to wait a little longer for the water to boil.

Is it somehow incomplete, the parting?

The steam began escaping from the kettle spout like a skein of white thread. The attached lid began clattering open and shut.

Is it deferred? The goodbye – or the closure? Indefinitely?

Outside the front door, the underbrush of the woods had turned almost black. The tree stumps – now covered in snow, their contours made round and powdery – shone faintly in the twilight.

Could I cut through that darkness? I wondered. Unlike the night before, I now had a torch. But more snow had piled up in the meantime. Even if I made it to the bus stop in one piece, the bus to P——, the nearest town, wouldn't be running. If I wanted to contact the hospital in Seoul where Inseon was staying, I would have to knock on doors wherever there was a light on and ask if I could use their phone. Could her sutured nerves have come undone? I wondered. Or perhaps she'd had the surgery, the one that involved cutting into her shoulder? Had the anaesthesia failed? Had there been some other medical mistake?

Inseon slid her right hand into her cotton glove, seemingly giving up hope of getting any answers out of me. She grabbed the handle of the kettle as it was clattering furiously, then filled the two mugs she'd placed on the workbench with the boiling water.

Remember how you worried? Inseon asked, sliding the first cup towards me. These weren't the wild mulberries. The tea was clear with a tinge of green and smelled of grass.

That there wouldn't be enough snow on Jeju? Inseon asked again with a grin, leaning against the workbench with her cup in one hand. I saw her press her smiling mouth to the rim, and wondered whether spirits could drink anything that hot.

What kind of tea is this? I asked.

Broadleaf bamboo.

I pressed my lips to the cup as well. As soon as I felt the tea making its way down my throat, I realized how much I had been waiting. To swallow something hot enough to scorch the tip of my tongue. To have that heat warm my throat and stomach.

When I was little, this is what we drank at home instead of water, said Inseon. I got sent to collect the canes of broadleaf bamboo that grow on the slopes, as they were supposed to be good for the nerves.

Inseon lowered her cup. When our eyes met, I wondered if the tea was spreading through her insides too. If Inseon had come to me as a spirit, that would mean I was alive, and if Inseon was alive, that would mean I was the apparition. Could the same warmth be spreading through both our bodies at once?

❧

I swung my head towards the woods. I'd heard a branch snap.

It's because there's no wind, Inseon said as if to put me at ease. With nothing to scatter the snow, the trees can't handle the weight.

The blue-grey twilight was illuminating the canopy. Large, luminous flakes continued to fall over the treetops.

I sipped some more tea. As it filled me with its warmth, my shoulders relaxed and my spine lengthened. Sitting up straight with the half-full cup still in my hand, I said, There's something I wanted to ask you too.

Inseon leaned forward from the edge of the workbench where she'd resumed her seat. As if to say she was listening.

How were you able to manage? I asked.

Inseon leaned in a little more.

By yourself, in this place.

She answered with a smile, What do you mean, this place?

I mean in a place with no street lamps or close neighbours. In a house where you're isolated and the power and water shut off when it snows. Where the tree at the back moves in on you through the night, swinging its menacing arms, and where just a stream away lie the remains of a village that was decimated and burned to the ground.

But as I didn't say any of that aloud, Inseon spoke instead, as if to gently refute what I'd said earlier. I'm not by myself, she told me.

A quiet gleam of affection lit up her face.

I have Ama.

The light faded from her eyes, then revived as scattered, forlorn embers.

Ami died a few months ago. Ama lived on nothing but water for three days afterwards. She wouldn't eat, not even the mulberries she likes so much.

Inseon paused for a moment.

Ami had been fine in the morning, but when I went back to the main house in the evening, his eyes were cloudy. I took him to the vet's right away, but he didn't make it past that day.

The twilight pouring into the woods was quickly darkening. The deeper that darkness grew, the more vividly the vents in the wood-burning stove glowed red.

I don't know why he hid his illness from me. I wasn't a predator he had to fear.

Inseon stared at the bright holes, as if staring hard enough at those gleaming eyes would make words flow out of the stove, hot like molten iron.

We had conversations, Ami and I — you saw us, Inseon said. She got down from the workbench.

Or could it be that we never actually communicated? Was he only ever a bird? Was I only ever a human in the end?

She slipped on her cotton glove again in an easy motion and opened the stove door. She poked at the burning firewood, sending up sparks. The warmth from the flames rushed across my face.

But that doesn't mean everything is over.

Inseon's voice mingled with the heat.

We haven't parted ways, not yet.

⌒

Not knowing how to comfort her, I gently asked a question. Where did you bury him?

Closing the stove door, now heated to a shade of scarlet, Inseon told me: In the yard.

Where in the yard?

Under the tree. She looked up at the windowless wall that faced the yard and said, The one you mistook for a person.

I realized then that I may have dug up the grave in the snow. I may have shattered the decaying bones with the shovel, and uprooted the brittle fragments with my clawing fingers.

⁓

When Inseon held her hand out, I thought for a moment she wanted to shake mine. But she was asking for my empty mug. Stacking them and setting them down on the workbench, she said, Let's leave these here for now.

Only then did I notice there had been no physical contact between us that day. Whenever we met up again after a long time apart, we would put our arms around each other in an embrace. We would greet each other – How long has it been? How are you doing? – while holding hands. Had we been keeping our distance without realizing it? As if the moment we touched, one of us might spread our death to the other.

Crossing the room towards the front door, Inseon turned her back to the blue-black snowscape outside and asked, Do you want some bean juk? I know that's one of your favourites.

She reached behind herself to shut the door. I found it hard to read her expression in the dark.

I turned to her as she secured the lock. Don't you have to soak the beans first? I asked.

I have some that I soaked and kept frozen. We can't use the blender with the power out, so it won't be as smooth, but it tastes good like that too.

Inseon strode past me towards the back door. I walked in her footprints, and amazingly managed to avoid bumping into any of the logs or timber or stepping in any blood. Before I followed her out of the door, I turned back to the stove. The two red vents on its heated side were still glaring.

When I got outside, the sky was darkening and Inseon was waiting for me under the snow. The flakes were floating down like feathers now, and I could see their crystalline shapes even in the vanishing twilight.

2

Shadows

Opening the front door with care, Inseon looked back at me. Finger to her lips, she told me, Ama's probably sleeping. Let's not wake her.

I stood outside the doorway and watched as Inseon, guided by the dim evening light, opened the shoe cabinet and felt around inside the shelves.

Where'd my lantern go? she murmured, crestfallen, before exclaiming under her breath, Ah! Here's a candle.

Inseon turned towards me and the doorway so that she could see better. She took a match out of a little matchbox, the kind that are given out for free. The match-head struck the side of the box and lit up with a hiss. Inseon transferred the flame to the wick of the candle and shook the match out.

Come in, she whispered, stepping out of her work shoes and on to the wooden floor.

I shut the front door and followed her inside. A soft shadow, not quite light but not completely dark either, was filtering in through the window. Thousands of snowflakes were drifting down, all bearing that shade.

I looked up at the lamp Ama had been swinging on earlier. Had she gone back inside her cage? Was she asleep as Inseon had said? If there's such a thing as falling asleep when you're dead.

Inseon was bent over the dining table, absorbed in the task of dripping candle wax on to its surface. When enough had amassed, she pressed the candle down and held it there, waiting for the wax to harden in a milky white crown around it.

Kyungha-ya. She called my name softly, not looking up. Would you mind covering up the birdcage?

I tiptoed over to the cage. The door was still ajar from when Ama had escaped. The cage held nothing but scattered grain husks and a half-full water dish. I grabbed the blackout cloth that was draped over the side of the table and tossed it over the empty cage.

She's fast asleep, isn't she? Inseon said.

I walked back to the kitchen. I sat down at the table, as if this were a regular evening and I'd simply happened to stop by a friend's house. Inseon too was rummaging through her freezer as though nothing were amiss. Like the only thing on her mind was how to throw together a dish for her unexpected guest.

I looked at the candle, observed how the flame soaked up the rippling pool of melted wax through the wick as it burned. Its fire was small and calm, not at all like the violent blaze inside the workshop stove. There was a bluish heart undulating deep within it. Like a seed with a beating pulse. Each pulse seemed to ripple out to its flickering orange edges.

I remembered how I'd reached my hand inside a flame once. A long-forgotten memory: in the autumn of my last year of elementary school, when our extracurricular teacher left the science lab for a moment after warning us to be careful with the equipment, one of my classmates said if we ran a finger really fast through the fire from an alcohol burner, we wouldn't feel a thing, neither heat nor pain. The kids who wanted to prove themselves brave lined up — some masking their fear, others unable to hide it — and touched the tips of their fingers to the fire before quickly yanking them back. When my turn came, I felt the fiery ribbon wrap around my finger with an unbelievable softness and a surging pressure. It was a fleeting sensation I knew I would not be allowed to savour, so to commit it to memory, I had to repeat the motion several times, each time a little faster. Before the sharp heat could pass through the dead skin cells and the epidermis and pierce the layers below.

I reached my hand out now, as if reliving the memory. That same unearthly softness immediately enveloped my skin. I was about to run my finger through the flame once more, when I caught a flash of movement in the central room and looked up.

⌣

It was the shadow of a bird, flying soundlessly over the white wall. The shadow was big, about as large as a six- or seven-year-old child. The details of its flexing wing muscles and translucent feathers were as vivid as if I were seeing them through a magnifying glass.

The only lighting in the house was the candle in front of me. To make that shadow, the bird had to be flying between the flame and the wall.

It's all right.

I turned my head towards Inseon's startlingly clear voice.

It's only Ami.

Inseon was standing with her back to the sink, and I noticed that she looked tired and about ready to collapse.

He doesn't always come, but it seems he did today.

The light of the candle barely reached Inseon's face. Her features were flattened by the dark, leaving her ashen and expressionless, a stranger.

Sometimes he's only here for a few seconds; other times he stays until the day breaks.

Inseon turned her back then, as if this were explanation enough. She tried the tap, muttering a barely audible complaint.

And the water's off too.

Outside the window, what faint illumination remained had vanished entirely. The flakes bearing the ashen blue light down to the ground were invisible now. Even the tree I had buried Ama under the night before, the same one Inseon had buried Ami under several months earlier, was lost to the pitch-black darkness.

That was when I heard it.

A sound like cloth brushing against cloth, like damp clods of soil crumbling between fingers. It was a sound that reminded me of Inseon. Not the Inseon standing beside me now, but the Inseon lying in the hospital room in Seoul, who had whispered in that low, static voice as though it were her vocal cords and not her hand that had been hurt.

I pushed the chair back and stood. I took a step towards the shadow, towards its direction-less beating wings that appeared to keep it eternally suspended, trapped between the rafters and the floor. I reached into the air between candlelight and shadow to where the bird's body should have been.

No.

The low intonations overlapped into a single word.

Was I hearing things? I wondered – and with that the word broke apart and scattered . . .
No, no.

The sound of cloth whispering against cloth

dragged the still-reverberating traces of the word into the night.

⁓

Inseon was sitting at the table now. The proximity of the candle added a sudden liveliness to her face, the flame animating her eyes. The fatigued woman leaning on the sink a moment ago was gone.

When I was here last autumn . . . I began, and saw the light vanish from her eyes. Ami kept saying *no* then too.

Inseon cupped her hands around the candle as if she were cold. Her hands reddened, absorbing the glow. The room around us grew dark as her hands covered the flame.

Did he learn the word from you? I asked.

Inseon splayed her fingers, and bright rays spilled out and stained her joints like blood.

I guess so, Inseon said. She pulled her hands away and the full flush of light enlivened her face.

Living alone, you get into the habit of talking to yourself, don't you? she said, nodding as if looking for agreement. I picked up this habit where, after I mumbled something, I would say 'no' in a louder voice, to take it back.

I hadn't pushed for an answer let alone asked her to elaborate, yet Inseon went on, choosing her words with care, as if she was obligated to answer me accurately.

Like how once we've let out words a spirit shouldn't hear or a wish they might actually heed and try to grant us . . . we rip up the paper we've written on.

Inseon's voice became firmer, like a pencil pressing down hard enough on paper to indent it.

So I guess that last word was what Ami heard most clearly. Who knows? Maybe he thought that was my animal cry and was simply mimicking me.

~

I didn't ask what her wish had been. I had a feeling I already knew. It was what I myself continued to battle. What I wrote down only to tear up each day. What was lodged in my sunken chest like an arrowhead.

Do you have a pencil?

Inseon fished a mechanical pencil out of her apron pocket and handed it to me. I took it and crossed the room, letting my shadow, which flickered with the wavering flame of the candle, lead the way. Nearing the wall, the gap between my shadow and the bird's narrowed. They appeared to touch, then one loosely overlay the other.

I reached out past my shadow with the hand that held the mechanical pencil. On the wall, I traced an outline of the bird's shadow, even as its head kept tilting, changing angles. I'd heard that birds did this to see the whole picture as they don't have binocular vision. What was the bird trying to see? Was there such a thing as wanting to see when all that remained of you was your shadow?

I didn't think I was pressing that hard, but the pencil lead kept breaking. With one hand on its cool surface, I moved slowly along the wall as I traced the line with my other hand, pressing the pencil cap at intervals to draw out new lead. When I reached the top of the bird's head, I had to stand on tiptoe and extend my arm as high as it would go. Then I discovered another line on the wall, drawn outside the one I was sketching now. The pencil outline I had left the previous autumn. I wasn't sure, but it looked like an outline of Ama's head. The long, gently sloping perimeter I had traced around the shadow cast by Inseon's shoulders was obscured by the bird's shadow. If I were to look at this wall come daylight, I realized, I wouldn't recognize any of the shapes in the criss-crossing and overlapping lines.

There was no more lead in the pencil. I turned back towards the kitchen with dread, feeling a stillness behind me where Inseon should have been sitting — a stillness that evoked the shrouded birdcage.

But I could make out Inseon's shoulders in the darkness. The low, measured breaths coming from the hush behind the candle's flame. Instead it was my own chair that stood chillingly empty.

Turning back to the wall, I saw that the bird's shadow was struggling as if to twist away from the traced line bounding it. The silhouette flared across the ceiling. Its wings opened out as if to take flight. *Cheep-cheep.* The faint call of a bird rang through the air, then died away.

Had Ama come back? I wondered, looking at the draped birdcage.

Where is Ama?

Returning to my seat, I saw that the candle on the table had shortened ever so slightly. A few cords of melted wax were running down its sides.

Sometimes . . . it feels like there's some other presence here, Inseon said, looking up from the knotted beads of wax. Like there's something that stays behind after Ami's come and gone.

Now a question followed, reaching me across the stillness.

Do you know what I mean?

As Inseon leaned forward, her shadow rippled across the ceiling. Sensing its movement, how it swelled and settled in time with her breathing, I answered with a question. How long have you felt that way?

I saw the familiar crease of her forehead, her usual look of concentration. Was she counting in months or in years? The clear melted wax pooled beneath the flame suddenly overflowed. It whitened instantly and formed new nodes down the pillar.

～

Ever since I saw the bones, Inseon answered. On the plane coming back from Manchuria.

This was unexpected. I'd thought she would say after Ami's death or after the loss of her mother. If it had started when she was filming in Manchuria, that was already ten years ago. Inseon was still living in Huam-dong back then.

That was the autumn they unearthed the remains, Inseon said.

Where? I asked.

She lowered her voice. Jeju Airport, she said. Underneath the runway.

I quietly met her eyes, which seemed to be asking if I remembered the event. I had forgotten the exact year, but I remembered seeing that article. And I remembered the photo of the pit in the ground, cordoned off with caution tape.

I'd grabbed a newspaper as I boarded the plane, she said, and there at the bottom of the front page was a photograph from the excavation site.

At some point, the wind had picked up – before the sound told me, the movement of the candlelight alerted me to it.

I looked back towards the room and saw that

the bird's shadow had disappeared. The wall on which I had outlined the movement of its head, perhaps because of the distance and darkness, appeared empty now.

I saw Inseon's eyes shift towards the wall. I was sure she would rise to her feet and stride over to the central room. To rip the cover off the cage and demand to know where Ama was. And why I'd failed to save her.

Instead, she raised her hands. She turned them over and slowly examined them, as if searching for a hidden wound or scar.

3

Wind

One set of remains by the wall of the pit caught my eye.

Mostly the bones suggested prone bodies lying face down in the dirt with sprawled legs, but this person seemed to have been on their side facing the wall. Their knees were drawn up to their chest, just as we curl up when we're unwell, or have trouble sleeping, or can't quieten our minds.

The article below the photo speculated that the victims were likely ordered to stand around the pit in groups of ten before being shot from behind and falling to their deaths. Then the next group would have been summoned, shot and so on.

I understood that the distinctive posture of this body suggested that the person was still breathing when they were buried beneath dirt. This would explain why the shoes remained on their feet. Based on the size of the rubber shoes and the overall skeletal frame, I imagined the body was that of a woman or a teenage boy.

Before I knew it, I'd folded up the newspaper and slipped it into my rucksack. Back home, I unpacked, made a clipping of the picture and tucked it away in a desk drawer. I opened the drawer only in broad daylight; I couldn't stomach the brutality of the scene at night. I would pore over the photo for a bit, then put it away. By winter, I got into the habit of lying under my desk and mimicking the posture.

I noticed how the temperature around me seemed to shift as I lay there. Not in the way a room warms as deep winter light wedges indoors or as ondol heat spreads beneath the floor, but in the way a warm build-up of gas fills a space. Much like the lingering soft feel of cotton, feathers or baby skin, but pressed, distilled and suffusing the room.

The idea of basing my next film on that person came to me as the year bled into the next. This person whose name, gender and age were unknown, who had been slight of frame and found wearing small gomusin on their feet, who numbered among the thousand who were preventively detained in Jeju as soon as the war broke out and were later shot dead.

They might have been a teenager, which would make them about the same age as my mother. So I wanted to focus on what awaited these two individuals in the aftermath: the sixty restless years spent beneath a runway that thundered with landing and departing planes, or here in this solitary house, with a coping saw tucked beneath her.

I decided to structure the film around my search for the identity of the unnamed deceased. I would visit the team of excavators with my clipping and ask them where the remains and the rubber shoes from the dig were being kept. I had read a few follow-up pieces that said close to fifty of the roughly one hundred dead found in the grave were being DNA-tested for potential familial matches, and kept in mind that my deceased could be among the fifty. In which case, interviewing the surviving relatives could turn out to be the next step.

But, first, I brought my camera down here to shoot a preliminary interview with my mum. I wanted to open the film with a low-key conversation about how the winter harvest was winding down and whether she was sleeping a bit better at night. I wouldn't expose her. I intended to frame her from the neck down and focus on her hands. There would only be one full shot of her in the whole film, of her sleeping over her rusted, concealed weapon, her back to the camera.

I caught an early flight down, then took the bus in and arrived here before noon.

Mum was in the village harvesting a mandarin hybrid at a neighbouring orchard, and, knowing she wouldn't be back until the evening, I spent some time preparing for the next day's interview. Looking for a good backdrop, I tried placing a chair by the lime-washed wall in the yard. I set up my camera and mic, sat down in the chair and started talking.

I wasn't thinking about the cave or my father. I rarely thought back to that time. I didn't understand why I was bringing it up now. But I couldn't stop, though the words didn't exactly pour out either. In the end, I stammered on beneath that wall until eventually the battery ran out. I repeated this a second time, then a third.

That night, I went to bed and realized things weren't going to plan. I didn't mention the interview to my mum. Instead I woke at dawn, got my head camera and walked over to the village I told you about before. The abandoned one across the dry stream.

It's a stone's throw from here and of course I'd

been to the stream countless times, though I'd never crossed it until that day. There weren't many of the old stone walls left standing in the village. I hadn't expected that. But it was easy to tell from the lack of trees where the houses and paths had been. Narrow footpaths were tucked in between the snug little lots. Some lots had soaring bamboo groves planted in the back, which suggested larger houses, especially for the time, had once stood there.

It was impossible to tell where my father had once lived.

Not without an address or a land registry map.

Not when I'd never been told how big his child-hood home had been nor on which side of the village it had stood.

～

There's a dull metallic clang as the wind knocks something over in the yard. It must be the shovel I left by the back door to the workshop. A large bead of wax runs down the candle as if in reac-tion to the vibrations.

As the sound of the gale picks up, the candle is re-energized. The flame leaps, as if there's an invisible object suspended between it and the ceiling that it is intent on setting ablaze. With a body as long as that, I could probably pass my whole hand through its fiery centre.

I listen to the chorus of rattling windows. The winds should have scattered the load weighing down the tree in the yard. Its fronds will be dancing in the air, jolted back to life. And in the woods outside the workshop, the larger trees whose trunks measure an arm span will be swaying too, as they slough their cover of snow.

⌒

That year, my father was nineteen.

He had three younger sisters ranging from twelve years old to an infant, and one younger brother. He doted on the baby sister, born that same year in early January. He was the one who named her Eunyoung, after dissuading my grandfather from calling her Soonyoung — her older siblings were named Hakyoung, Sookyoung, Jinyoung and Heeyoung. She's a lamb as it is, he said, why risk making her more docile with a name like Soon?

He had a windbreaker with an elastic waistband that my grandmother had got for him to wear with his winter uniform. During the student strike that spring, when he went home to save on boarding-house fees, he got into the habit of tucking his baby sister inside that jacket. He liked to lower the zip and show off her soft velvety hair to his friends, and listen to the girls gush when she wrapped her tiny fist around his collar. My grandmother scolded him, said he was bound to drop her, but he told her not to worry; he always had a good hold on her. And if he ever fell, he'd make sure to fall on his back so the baby would be right as rain.

My grandparents were worried sick about their eldest son, as he was the only man at home within the age range the soldiers and police were likely to suspect of communicating with the guerrillas in the hills. There were widespread rumours about how police who spoke the northern dialect raided villages and hauled young men away to be counted towards their arrest numbers. Detectives who had once worked for the Japanese Higher Police remained on the force and went on torturing people as they had done before liberation. After learning about a high-school student who died after being tortured at a police station, my grandfather sent my father to hide in the caves by himself. My father would light his little porcelain oil lamp to read and study during the day — he dreamed of applying to a college in Seoul once things had quietened. Before the sun set, he made sure to put out the light and would sit through the darkness. He would wait until midnight to steal home, eat the food that had grown cold and briefly nod off. Then, well before first light, he would creep back up to the cave with some steamed potatoes and salt he'd wrapped up in a twist of paper.

That November night, he was heading back up as usual and was crossing the dry stream bed when he heard whistles and saw the woods turn bright. The houses were burning.

His instinct told him to remain where he was. He hid in a bamboo grove at the edge of the stream. Then he heard gunshots, seven in total, coming from the vacant lot in their village. Through the trees he watched soldiers with whistles jostle people out of the village. He was quite far away, but he spotted two of his siblings among the crowd. They were holding hands. Women walking behind even younger children or with infants on their backs as well as elders kept falling over or dawdled, slowing down the line. Soldiers blew their whistles and brandished their guns to push them along.

As soon as he was sure they were gone, my father

ran down to the village. He looked behind him and saw that the more populated lower half of their village was also ablaze. The fire was so big and bright he said he could see white clouds above the smoke.

Only the walls enclosing the houses and fields and the masonry of the stone houses were spared. My father reached their own yard and was stunned to find it smeared in red, until he realized the gochujang pots had burst. He searched the house and, finding no one inside, rushed down to the hackberry tree in the village lot. There were seven people lying dead. One of them was my grandfather. The soldiers had visited each home with copies of the resident register and, insisting that any male member of the family not present must have joined the rebels, they had executed the remaining family members.

My father carried my grandfather's body on his back and brought him to their yard. He gathered an armful of bamboo leaves and laid them like cloth over his father's face and body, then dragged out the metal head of a burned shovel from the heap of smouldering embers that was all that remained of their shed. He waited for the metal to cool, then covered the leaves with dirt.

The candle's orange flame is tall, supple, alive. Inseon keeps her eyes on it.

None of this is included in the film, she says.

I nod. It's true. Sitting in front of that lime-washed wall, all she touches on in the film is the darkness she'd seen in the cave, the footsteps in the snow that were erased within seconds.

Mum didn't tell me any of this until right before her memory started to fade, so I wasn't even aware of it at the time.

I feel a hint of the wind's force on my cheeks and along the blade of my nose. The darkened lampshade above the table sways slowly. The taut, upright flame shrinks, like it's about to be extinguished. I can almost sense a presence outside embracing the house. The cold mass of its breath winding through the rafters and every single opening in the house.

It only took a week for my father to be caught, Inseon says, lifting her eyes from the burning light.

He couldn't survive on condensation off the cave walls alone; he had to find food. He came down to look for grain that hadn't burned, and ran right into them. The cops were lying in wait for when people would return to bury the dead.

Do you think he got to see his family then? I ask, but Inseon shakes her head.

That wasn't possible, as the military and police each had their own chain of command. He was locked up in the old alcohol factory by the port for a fortnight, then sent across to Mokpo. The mainland police were waiting at the wharf and informed him on the spot of his sentence and where he was to be imprisoned.

The shadows cast by the candle's glow are constantly in motion and I can't tell if Inseon's expression is changing moment to moment or if it's only the light and shadow fluctuating.

What about the people the soldiers rounded up?

They were held in an elementary school in P— for a month, then in December, on the white sands since made into a public beach, they were all shot dead.

All of them?

All except the immediate family of any of the soldiers or police.

Including infants?

Extermination was the goal.

Exterminate what?

The reds.

～

The front door judders again like someone's pounding on it. The low flame, shorter even than the wick, swells again. Inseon remains impassive. She places her palms on the table: ten neat fingers in a row. Pressing down on their tips, she rises from the table.

I have something to show you, she says.

～

I watch Inseon walk over to the open door of her room. From the yard there's another loud clatter amid the flapping of tarp, the shrill moan of the wind. Inseon glides through it all. Her movement is slow, steady, silent, like she's feeling her way forward using tendrils rather than relying on her vision.

She reappears shortly with one of the boxes she keeps on her iron shelf. I wonder how she found it in the dark. Simply from memory? Inseon places the box next to the candle and removes the lid with both hands. There's a stack of books and booklets marked with yellow Post-its and light and dark green flags. The Post-its have dates and headwords written on them. Inseon places the books in an orderly fashion on the table. I notice a framed black-and-white photo at the bottom of the box that she hasn't bothered to remove. It's about the size of my palm and shows a young man and woman wearing a suit and dress. A studio portrait.

I quickly realize that the woman on the stool is Inseon's mother. I'd thought her a girlish older woman when I met her and had briefly imagined a delicate face, but the photo shows an affable young woman whose small figure exudes poise and pep. Of the two, it's the lean man, standing beside her with his hand on her shoulder, who appears delicate. I take note of his clear porcelain features, his large, single-lidded eyes that seem to glisten. Inseon has inherited her father's eyes and physique, I conclude, but in all other aspects she takes after her mother in her youth.

⁓

Inseon runs a finger over the spines of the stacked books. The one she picks out is subtitled 'Secheon-ri' and numbered 12, and it's not unfamiliar to me. I'd come across the series of books in winter 2012, while I was in the stacks of the National Library researching my book on G—. At the time, I was reading up on related or similar instances of historical mass killings both at home and abroad in preparation for my book on the subject. But I'd resolutely passed over these volumes, which contained the oral history of the massacres perpetrated in villages across this island. The six-hundred-page fact-finding report, other relevant introductory material, the testimonies of some thirty people in the appendices – I had found them altogether too overwhelming.

Inseon opens it to a page marked with a

light green flag. She turns the book round and
offers it to me.

*No better view of it than from our place here. Look
over yonder. You see sea, sands, all of it, from this
maru right here. That day too, saw it all from my
room. Poked a hole in the window paper as I was too
afraid to open the sliding door.*

It's dark and the printed text is small. I place the
book right beneath the candle and push my face
close to the page to continue reading. The book
smells musty from all the water it has absorbed
and released over years of rainy seasons.

*At sundown, two truckfuls of folk were brought over.
At least a hundred. Soldiers drew a square on that
sand there with those bayonets they carry. Told folk,
go stand inside it. Stand straight, no sitting, keep to
your row, it looked like they were shouting, but the
wind carried the sound out to sea. They kept blowing
their whistles, though, but once folk were standing
quiet inside the lines, they stopped.*
    *Some high-ranking person, a soldier, barked out
an order, and ten of the folk walked out from the
square and stood neat-like, facing the sea. I watched*

to see what punishment was coming, but the soldiers shot them from behind without warning and all ten of them fell face first into the water. They ordered another group to form a queue, but no one wanted to step forward and the rows got messed up. The soldiers pointed their guns and yelled at folk to stand straight, and that's when a handful of them at the back jumped the perimeter and made a run for it, right towards us.

I was twenty-two, my eldest barely a hundred days old. Soldiers began shooting this way, so I held my baby close and pulled a blanket over our heads. His abang had just joined the Minbodan and was down at the police station on duty every day until dark. So it was just the little one and me, and . . . I've never heard so much gunfire in all my life, not then and not since. After a long while, everything grew quiet and I crept over, I was shaking so hard, to the door, to peek out of the hole I'd made, and they were all dead on the sand, every last one. The soldiers picked them up by their shoulders and feet and threw them in the ocean, and I swear they looked like clothes floating on the waves.

❧

This book doesn't have photographs, but I found one in here, Inseon tells me.

She opens a booklet about the size of a *Reader's Digest* to a page marked with a Post-it. I check the date written in black ink on the yellow sticky note. Autumn, fifteen years ago.

The black-and-white image shows an elderly woman with short curly hair that's gone mostly grey sitting on the narrow maru out front, mending a fishing net. She is in profile and, from her gruff look, I gather she didn't consent to having her full portrait taken. Perhaps because this is a news article and not an interview transcript, I notice that beneath the photo a pull quote of the woman's words has been translated into standard Korean.

I don't eat sea meat. Back then, things being as bad as they were, there were no harvests, and with an infant on my hands, I had to eat whatever I could to keep my milk flowing and keep my baby fed. But once things got better, to this day, I haven't eaten a bite of anything from the water. Sea critters are what ate away at those people, aren't they?

The thin, glossy paper reflects the candlelight and brightens the page, and the article itself is in larger print and easier to read. I skip through most of it and read only the quoted bits. Mostly they repeat the interview testimony, but occasionally new elements crop up.

I was afraid the bullets would reach my room, so I hid under a blanket and listened to the gunfire. All the while my heart wouldn't stop trembling for the children I'd seen out on the sands. There were women holding babies as young as my son, and one woman looked like she'd give birth any day. I saw how she supported her back with her hands as she stood. It was growing dark when the guns stopped. I peeked out of the door again. The soldiers were hurling bodies into the ocean, and people lay bloodied, their faces in the sand. At first I thought they were clothes floating on the water, but it turned out they were all people, dead people. Early the next day, while his father slept, I sneaked down there with my son on my back. I looked everywhere, sure I'd find an infant swept back to shore, but I found nothing. There had been so many people, but now there wasn't so much as a stitch of clothing or a single shoe. The spot where they'd done the killing had been washed clean by the tide. There wasn't a trace of blood. So that's why they chose to kill them here, I thought.

Inseon reaches for the heaviest tome on the table. Based on its relatively sophisticated design, I guess that it was likely published within the last decade.

This is her last interview, Inseon says as she cracks the book open to a page marked with a bright orange sticky flag. There's a colour photo of an elderly woman, the same woman, whose hair is now as hoary as the plumage on white birds. Her flesh and muscle have atrophied and she is so diminished she is almost unrecognizable. She sits on the same wooden deck at the front of the house with her knees bent and her feet flat on the ground, her back against a column. The only vitality I can detect is in her eyes, which are open towards the camera.

⌒

Didn't I tell you to stop coming? I've said all I have to say – why do you keep coming back?

What I haven't told anyone?
What is there I haven't told . . .

It started with those research folk. There weren't many who saw it with their own eyes, they said, and asked me to tell them, said if I didn't get it off my chest before I died, no one would ever know. I figured that wasn't wrong, so I told them that very day. That was the first time. Once I did though, others kept coming. They'd get me talking, then they'd leave, and I'd be turned inside out for days of course. I knew what it'd do to me, and still, as much as I could, I did as they asked.

If my husband were alive he'd have hated it, but he'd died all those years ago; he couldn't stop me. What could he do? Chase after me from the beyond? If ghosts were real, he might have visited me in my dreams to stop me, but he hasn't yet.

My husband didn't suffer much harm during the troubles. He fought in the war, sure, had that brush with death, but that's all. A lot of folk from Jeju joined the navy then. Stay on the island and you'd either be dragged away and killed by the military or the police, or if you were Minbodan and followed the cops around, you'd have to see all kinds of heinous things you couldn't unsee: those were the choices. The sooner you stepped off this island, the sooner you could rest easy; that's why my husband was the first to join voluntarily. Then not a peep for three years — Was he dead? Was he not? — until one day he was back. He said he'd been lucky but so many of the folk from Jeju had died fighting. Said it was really, really hard to lie low, what with all the talk about Jeju folk all being reds.

What did he do before the war? When he was following the soldiers and cops around? How would I know when he never told me? I know it wasn't by choice that he went with them. He was out building a defence wall with the villagers when the cops came and picked out some men to go with them. It was a different time then. You had to do as you were told.

The Seocheong were merciless; there were rumours that they would just as easily kill off the militia folk who accompanied them and did their bidding, so I worried of course. I heard about how after stabbing the bride of one of the men hiding out in the hills with bayonets, they dumped her in the yard outside the nearest police station and told the militia to jab their bamboo spears in her. When I reminded him not to get on anyone's bad side, my husband always said, I'm only there to interpret. The Seocheong didn't under-stand Jeju-mal, and Jeju folk didn't understand the Seocheong. During the sokai — *evacuation — when they went around burning the upland villages, my husband swears all he did was knock on doors and tell folk, Everything's on fire, leave now. It was strange, though, how he wouldn't pick up our baby after that day, not once, not even when he joined the navy. I'll spread my uncleanliness if I touch him, I'm not even supposed to look him in the eyes, he used to say, and never so much as glanced at the child.*

My husband never spoke ill of the military or the police, not for as long as he lived. He didn't breathe a word about them, good or bad. The reds he couldn't stand, though. What did those rebels ever do, he'd say, except kill some cops and take revenge on inno-cent families, then run and hide in the hills while two or three hundred souls were slaughtered in retali-ation in their villages alone? All to build their earthly paradise, but what kind of paradise is hell?

So I didn't breathe a word about that day, not even to him. What could I say to someone who crept in at night quiet as a mouse to curl up on the unheated side of the floor with his back turned?

I only ever spoke about it once. Just the one time, then not a word until those researchers showed up. Our baby son was in middle school by then, so it was a good fifteen years after the troubles.

It was that time of year when by morning and night there's a chill in the air, but the sun still beats down.

I was hanging red chillies out to dry by the gate when a stranger approached. He had a polite manner about him and said, if I didn't mind, he wanted to ask if we'd lived here before the war.

This was during the military revolution, mind you, when no one so much as whispered about that earlier time. I could easily have said that we'd moved here from somewhere else, but I've never been canny like that and I can't tell a lie, and besides it didn't look like he was an official — from his eyes and his voice, I thought he like as not wouldn't hurt a fly, so I told him to come inside. I had him sit on the doorstep and left the gate open as he wasn't family, then I asked him in a low voice, so as no one could hear, why was he here and what did he want to know? At that, the man became all apologetic. He was so sorry to show up out of the blue like this, he didn't mean to be a nuisance or cause any trouble. Aieee, who has the patience for all that? I said it was fine, told him to get to his question. So the man finally opens his mouth, and he asks, Did you see children on the beach that day?

At those words, I couldn't breathe — it was like a box iron was sitting over the pit of my stomach here, below my breastbone. I'd done nothing wrong, I don't know why my eyes got blurry, my mouth all dry. I knew I should say I had no idea and get him to leave, but for some reason I wanted to answer. It felt like I'd been waiting for him. Like I'd been waiting those fifteen years to have someone ask me that very question.

So I told him the truth. Yes, there were children there. My heart was pounding like it might burst, my words came out in a stammer, but by now he was all calm and collected, and he sat quietly for a good while before asking again if I'd maybe heard a baby cry.

He was a stranger — my husband would be furious if he found out — and still I answered. Like I was half out of my body. I didn't hear any crying, I said, but I did see women holding babies. Because I did — three women with infants tight in their arms, standing in the box the soldiers had scratched out. And seven or eight children huddling together, children around four and seven years old, ten at the most. I saw them look up at the women and move their lips sometimes, but the wind was seawards and I couldn't make out what they were saying or shouting.

The man didn't move and wouldn't say a word, so I figured he had no more to ask. Eventually, though, he spoke again. He asked me if a baby had turned up on the shore. If not on that day, then on the day after, or in the weeks after.

But I didn't have the strength left to talk . . . Why was he here? I wanted to ask. Why these questions after all this time? But I couldn't get the words out. Finally I managed to say in a whisper that no one had turned up — and that was when I saw how his shirt was soaked in sweat, from the collar all the way down his back.

I went to the kitchen and brought him a bowl of water. But the man wouldn't accept it. His hands were on his lap but they were shaking so much he would've knocked the bowl over if he tried to take it. He knew this — that was why he wasn't even trying. And now that I knew too, I couldn't take the bowl away, that would have been heartless, so I stood there with my arm out for a good while.

But the young ones would be back from school and I needed him gone before then. If my husband heard about it, there would be such a row. I went back to the kitchen, put the bowl down and rubbed my chest a few times. When I came back out, the man was gone. Not a trace of him ever being there. I sat down on the doorstep and looked out at the steel sea. I thought I might hear his footfall again at any moment, but I couldn't tell if I was waiting or if I was petrified.

4

Stillness

I look up and am startled by the darkness. While reading, my nose buried in the book, I'd forgotten where I was. The wind too had died down without my noticing. I stare up at the dark window, swathed in such a deep hush that all its earlier rattling now seems a thing of the distant past. In the sudden lull, I feel as if I've opened the door to a dream within a dream and stepped inside.

The candlelight has stopped flickering. The blue seed of the flame's core is staring me in the eyes. The candle is down to half a finger. Several strands of wax have run over the sides and on to the table, hardening like strings of beads.

Sitting crouched across the table from me, Inseon says, I've been to her place too.

When?

The year before last. Only the woman's son and daughter-in-law were living there.

Her answer is laboured, as if with each word her tongue is straining against the silence.

In the winter of the same year she gave this interview, she passed away.

More candle wax spills over into new strings.

There was one thing the woman had misunderstood.

Inseon turns towards the central room as she says this, and I follow her gaze. All I can see beyond the half-open sliding door is darkness.

My father's hands weren't shaking because he was emotional, she says.

She places her fist against her chest, right over her heart.

He used to heat up a stone a little wider than my fist and place it here, then sit on the bedroom floor with his back against the wall. He said he could breathe better sitting up.

I study the raised blue veins on Inseon's pale fist where it rests over her black parka. A fist that looks more like a heart than a stone.

When his stone had cooled, gone lukewarm, my father would call for me. I would bring the stone to the kitchen, where my mother would boil it in a pot of water. I remember watching until bubbles rose from the little holes pockmarking it.

My mother would drain the pot, wrap the stone in a dishcloth and give it to me to take back to my father.

Inseon lowers her fist. She places it gently on the table, as if she is setting down a heart.

Did he have a heart problem?

He took medicine for angina, she replies evenly. Had a heart attack in the end. The tremor in his hands too was an after-effect of the torture.

⌣

Inseon unclenches her fist, slowly folding the booklets shut and hiding them away.

How long has she been collecting these?

If she went to visit that house by the sea the year before last, she must have started on this even earlier. It would have been easy enough to consult the materials and check them out from the provincial library or the Jeju 4.3 Research Institute, but to obtain them personally would have taken a lot more effort. To find the magazines that hadn't been digitized, she would have had to scour second-hand bookshops or contact the publishers in Seoul to request back issues.

Not that this sort of thing would have been hard or new for her. She had always done her own research, as she did her own casting, over the decade she spent producing films on shoestring budgets.

Is she working on a film? I wonder – perhaps she's prepping to reshoot or add on to her last one?

⌒

I start to ask her if this is the case, but Inseon's face hardens before I finish the question.

That's not something I've considered.

With her elbows on the table, she lowers her chin to her clasped hands in a gesture that reminds me of the elderly woman in the photo. The deep frown lines between her brows and her stubborn expression are almost identical to how she looked at her most recent director's talk. Inseon's last film, which hadn't been all that well received, had screened with a favourable blurb written by the film festival organizer attached to it as a sort of subtitle: 'An ode in film to a father's history'. Inseon had rejected this characterization. It's not a film for my father, she said. And it's not a film about history, and it's not an ode in film. The host seemed surprised, but smiled and returned smoothly, Then what is the film about? I don't recall what Inseon said in response. But whenever my thoughts came back to what might have prompted her to quit making films, that moment was what I remembered. The host's blend of astonishment, curiosity and coldness, the confused silence from the audience, Inseon's face as she slowly pieced together her words, like someone doomed to only ever speak the truth.

Our project is the only project I've considered in the last four years, says Inseon, unclasping her fingers and lowering her hands. She's about to add something else, but this time I stop her.

We decided not to do that project, Inseon.

She looks unconvinced, which I imagine was the same expression she wore last summer when I said as much over the phone.

I told you I'd been wrong from the start. That I'd been thinking about it too simply.

Inseon doesn't refute this right away, instead closing her eyes as if trying to gather her thoughts.

She opens her eyes again and asks calmly, What do you make of it now, then?

In that moment, as though someone has flicked a switch, my dream roars back, so vivid and tangible I stop breathing for a second. The squishing of my trainers, the sponginess of the ground underfoot, the water seeping up from beneath the snow. The tide rising up to my knees in the time it would take to blink, engulfing the black tree torsos, the burial mounds.

I say quietly, Dreams are terrifying things. No — they're humiliating. They reveal things about you that you weren't even aware of.

Even as I say this, I'm thinking what a strange night this is. I'm confessing to something I've never told a soul.

Like how those nightmares ransacked my life night after night, I tell her. How I have no one left, no one alive who is by my side any more.

That's not true, Inseon says, cutting me off. It's not true that you have no one left.

Her tone is firm, which makes her seem angry, her bright eyes flashing as they bore into mine.

. . . You have me.

This time, I'm the one who closes my eyes. Because a quiet pain unmoors me at the thought that I might now be losing Inseon too.

When we met as twenty-four-year-olds, Inseon was already two years out of a two-year college where she'd earned a photography degree. She had two years on me in the workforce and appeared more responsible and capable than I was in almost every way. I never told her this, but on occasion I saw her almost as an older sister. The first time was when we visited Wol-chulsan and I felt unwell before we'd even started our hike. This was to be the third site in our feature on the more renowned mountains across the country and their surrounding villages, and I was having my stomach spasms. Inseon found me some painkillers and antispasmodics at the lone pharmacy in the town of Yeongam and handed them to me with a plain yoghurt and a plastic spoon.

The pharmacist suggested Gelfos, she said, but I thought antacids might make the nausea worse, so I got you this instead.

Even after eating the yoghurt and taking the medicine, I suffered all night, and when we ended up having to cancel our plans the following day,

Inseon said in her easy-going way, Why don't we go home and come back on Saturday? I won't file the travel expenses this time. I'll just count this as a personal trip with a friend gone awry.

At dawn the following Saturday, Inseon spotted me at the train station and waved with abandon, like we really were friends. We unpacked our bags at our lodgings in town and set out for our hike, but as soon as we arrived at Windy Pass, Inseon found a spot to set up her tripod from which we had a gorgeous view of the rambling trails, then brought out the simple gimbap she'd prepared for us. As with all Inseon's cooking, as I've since discovered, the gimbap was plain and a little bland. She'd rolled it with just three fillings — cucumber, carrot and burdock root.

Once we had finished our gimbap, we sat for a bit. Inseon asked me, What would you do?

At first, I didn't understand the question.

If you were that woman, she added.

We had been discussing the fact that each of the three mountains we had visited so far had a rock with a story behind it. Each legend followed an almost identical pattern. An old drifter shows up at a mountain village and knocks on every

door for a meal, only to be turned away by everyone save for a lone woman who offers him a bowl
of food. As a show of gratitude, the drifter tells
the woman to make sure to go up the mountain
before daybreak the next morning without telling anyone where she is going. She is not to look
back until she has crossed over to the other side
of the mountain. The woman does as the man
says, and when she is halfway up the mountain, a
tidal wave or torrential downpour submerges the
village whole. In every story, without exception, the woman looks back. She turns to stone
on the spot.

This was around the end of May, when the
days had grown noticeably longer. Inseon sat
perched on a wide rock, the sleeves of her cotton-
hemp shirt rolled up to her elbows, as she
repeatedly clamped a cigarette between her teeth,
chewed on it a bit, then slipped it back into the
pack without ever lighting it – she was a chain-
smoker throughout her twenties, though she
would later quit at thirty. A fire-weather alert was
in effect and she was being careful.

If she hadn't turned round, she would have
been free . . . If she'd only crossed the mountain.

Listening to Inseon's playful grousing, I

thought back to the rocks we saw on our first and second trips. Each as slender as a statue, each once a stepdaughter, a daughter-in-law, a serf, a persecuted woman in the world below – they all had looked behind them and transformed into rock.

I asked back, When do you think they turned to stone? The moment they looked back? Or do you think it took a little more time?

We came down the mountain before it grew dark, and once we returned to our room on the second floor and opened the window to draw in fresh air, I thought back to our conversation, which we had left off with those questions. It came to mind when I looked out and caught a glimpse of the stone woman on the mountainside, her back to the setting sun.

The woman appeared before me, a woman startling at the sight of her own feet turning to stone. But as only her feet had petrified, she could turn round and continue up the mountain still. So she trudges ahead a few more steps before turning back again, and this time her calves harden into rock. Lugging her heavy legs forward, she resumes her climb up the slope. If she makes it over the mountain pass, she may survive, as long as she doesn't look back. But she does – she turns her head. Once the stone has overtaken her from her knees up to her stomach, there is nothing more she can do. She stands there until the flood-waters that had inundated the houses and covered the tops of all the trees recede. Until her pelvis and her heart and her shoulders become stone. Until enough of her wide-open eyes has been overrun by rock that they no longer appear bloodshot. And now she stands, under rain and snow, through countless cycles of the sun and moon. And for what? What had she kept turning back to see?

Inseon walked over to the window after plugging in her batteries and chargers and organizing her travel bag.

They say she turned to stone, not that she died, right? she said. She lit a cigarette, sucked in the blue smoke and blew a long stream of it out of the window.

She might not have died then, Inseon went on. Maybe that rock . . . is like a husk. Shed skin turned to stone. Her eyes flashed mischievously.

Ah, now that I've said it, I think it might be true, she said, looking serious but switching to familiar speech without warning. The woman shed her skin and took off!

I smiled at Inseon as she waved her hands in triumph. For where? I asked.

Well, wherever she wanted to go. She crossed the mountain and started a new life, or she plunged head first into the water, or . . .

By now we were both speaking familiarly, and we never went back to formal speech after that day.

Into the water?

Yeah, I bet she dived right in.

Why?

There must've been someone she wanted to save. Isn't that why she looked back?

Since that evening, Inseon and I have been friends. We went through all our life milestones together, right up until she moved back to the island. Not long after I quit working at the magazine, around the time I buried my parents and holed up in the empty flat, she began messaging me at odd moments to tell me she was dropping by. *Just do one thing for me? Let me in.* And when

I did, she would wrap her arms around my shoulders, along with a rush of cold wind and the smell of cigarettes.

◡

When I open my eyes, the silence and the darkness are still waiting, unchanged.

It feels as though invisible snowflakes fill the space between us. As though the words we've swallowed are being sealed in between their myriad melded arms.

◡

A line of smoke like a single black thread curls up from the tip of the burning wick. I watch until the wisp disperses, vanishing into thin air. Scenes of soldiers holding up lit pine torches to the eaves of stone houses flash before my eyes.

Was this house also burned down? I ask Inseon.

It occurs to me that they could have come here too, the night they set the houses on the other side of the stream ablaze. *Everything's on fire, leave now.* Had they stormed through the yard, whistles shrilling, and pounded on the door?

Who lived here back then? I ask.

Had they slashed that sliding door open with their bayonets? Who would have been inside when they did?

This house belonged to my mum's side of the family, Inseon answers. My great-grandmother lived here with her eldest son and his wife, but as soon as they were ordered to evacuate, they fled to the home of a distant cousin who lived near the sea, just barely avoiding an encounter with the soldiers. They were lucky they had a place to go.

Of course, she adds, this house was burned down that night too. Only the stone walls remained. The rest had to be rebuilt.

⁓

We're sitting where the flames once spread.

We're sitting where the beams fell in and sent clouds of ash rising into the air.

⁓

Inseon stands, her shadow soaring to the ceiling. It swells and shrinks with her movements as she puts the booklets back inside the box and closes the lid.

Should we head to my room? she asks.

She doesn't wait for me to answer. *What to do about the candle?* she mumbles, as if she's sure I will accompany her.

Inseon goes to the sink and comes back with a paper cup in one hand and a pair of scissors in the other. She cuts an X into the bottom of the cup. She prises the candle from the spot where the hardened wax has glued it in place and sets it inside the cup, the white coating softening the light that shines through.

Let's go, she says.

I don't move.

There's something I want to show you, she says.

Her shadow, nearly twice her size, wavers on the white ceiling as it moves towards my own.

When I push my chair back and stand up, it's because I want that shadow to stop. Because I refuse to let it spread like ink and engulf my own.

I reach out and tuck my hands under the box. Feeling its solid heft, I lift it up and hold it to my chest. Inseon leads the way, candle in hand. Our bodies aren't touching, but our shadows, which resemble a pair of giants joined at the shoulders, quiver as they dance across the ceiling.

She steps inside, past the opaque glass pane in the frame of the sliding door with its ornate pattern of repeating blocks and bars resembling the character 亞. Before following her, I look back. The darkness of the central room and kitchen in the absence of the candlelight is like the black depths of the sea. As I walk into the room that ripples with the flame's shadows, I feel I am entering a cabin at the bottom of a shipwreck, a small pocket of air underwater. I shut the door with my shoulder, as if to stop a rush of water from surging in.

⌣

I walk up to where Inseon stands facing the iron bookcase.

As she slowly moves the candle along the shelves, the black scribbles on the Post-it notes affixed to each box appear to stir under the flame. Inseon's penmanship is both hurried and precise. The strokes flow with confidence even as the characters remain legible. I read these characters, which seem to swell like voices under the light, only to fall silent once the candle passes. They mostly designate place names and years. Some names are of people, likely those who gave the testimonies, and some of the numbers seem to mark their birth years.

Here, Inseon says, and I push the box into the empty slot on the shelf. Inseon bends down and the sudden arc of the candlelight as her arm drops to the lower shelves gives me vertigo. Like the ship is lurching and the boxes will come tumbling down on me.

Can you hold this?

I take the candle from her, and she stoops lower still. She runs her fingertips along the variously sized boxes on the bottom shelf as if rummaging through wreckage. The motion is familiar, practised, and I realize this is the answer to my earlier question by the woodstove. How she's managed by herself, in this place. What she's been doing all these years.

Inseon takes a box halfway off the bottom shelf, removes the lid and pulls out a large map. She opens the thrice-folded map and spreads it out on the floor, crouching down on one knee.

This is the school my mother went to, in Hanjinae, she says.

I lower one knee to the floor too and shine the light over the tiny circle – no bigger than a grain of rice – Inseon is indicating. There's a map symbol for a school printed inside it, so a school must still be there.

Where is this house on the map?

Here.

Inseon finds a spot that's higher up than I was expecting, inside dense, brown contour lines.

And this is where my mother lived.

She points to a tiny mark made with a felt tip, right by the location of the school.

Placing her index and middle fingers on the two adjacent dots, Inseon says, My mum told me before that she probably wouldn't have gone if the school had been far away. This was back when families were willing to pay for lodgings in town if that meant their sons could attend the middle school there, while daughters were left uneducated. When the neighbours chided my grandmother, asking her why she'd go to the trouble of educating all three of her daughters, she replied with a smile, *The world's a-changing*. And knowing their mother wouldn't give them chores as long as they were studying, my mum and her little sister would drag out their assignments for hours.

Inseon's fingernail, cut to the quick, traces a long, slow curve above the village.

The evacuation order was for the areas five kilometres from the shore, so it didn't apply to Hanjinae, which fell right outside the line. Preoccupied by thoughts of her mother, brother and his wife being treated as unwelcome guests at the distant cousin's home, my grandmother sent her two older daughters down to the coast, to take rice and potatoes to the cousin. Inseon's finger hovers over a black dot near the ocean that must mark the location of that home.

It was a ten-ri road down to the coast and my uncle, twenty years old at the time, said he would go with his sisters and carry the load, but my grandfather stopped him from going, saying it was dangerous for young men to be out and about. Their baby sister was eight years old and insisted on going with my mum and aunt, had gone and washed up and got dressed all by herself to do just that, but my grandmother put her foot down. Wasn't the little one bound to walk in zigzags and beg her sisters to carry her the rest of the way before they'd even gone five ri?

⌒

This next part, I've told you once before. Do you remember?

As soon as Inseon says this, the details of that night come back to me. The roads and pavements were blanketed in untrodden snow. Layered white mounds of it rested atop standing signs and outdoor air-conditioning units, on worn windowsills. While the flakes burrowing into my trainers were spine-tinglingly cold, there was an unbelievable softness to the snow underfoot, and with each step I couldn't tell whether I was feeling pain or pleasure.

There were things I left out of that story. Things I misunderstood too.

Inseon pores over the black mark on the map as if it were a well, as if she sees something reflected on the dark surface of the water inside.

When the two sisters came back to the village, the bodies weren't in the schoolyard at the elementary school but in the barley field opposite the school gates, under a smattering of snow. The pattern is the same in almost every village. They'd round up people in a schoolyard, then butcher them in a nearby field or by the water.

It must be my imagination playing tricks on me, but I think I see the tiny dot on the map briefly stir. Like an insect that plays dead, then scurries off the moment you look away.

They wiped the snow off the frozen faces, one by one, until they finally found their parents, but there was no sign of their brother or their baby sister nearby. My mum and aunt hoped the young men of the village had seen the soldiers coming and fled in time – their brother was fast and always ran the last leg in relay races – but they couldn't understand the absence of their baby sister and became anxious. They searched amid the hundred or so dead bodies in the field once more, nudging some of them aside to see whether their sister lay pinned beneath. It was close to dusk when, as a last resort, they went back to where their home had once stood.

That's where they found her.

At first, my mother thought someone had dropped a heap of red rags in the yard. My aunt felt around beneath their little sister's blood-soaked jacket and found a bullet hole in her stomach. When my mother pushed aside the girl's hair, stiff with blood and clinging to her face, she found another bullet wound in her sister's lower jaw. The bullet had shattered part of her jawbone on its way out. The matted tangle of her hair must have been stemming the flow of blood, and now the wound began to bleed afresh.

My aunt removed her own jacket and tore off both sleeves with her teeth, wrapping the fabric round each wound as a tourniquet. The two older sisters took turns carrying the unconscious youngest on their backs all the way to the distant cousin's house. When the three of them arrived, smeared in blood as though they'd stepped in red-bean juk, the adults simply stared.

Because of the curfew, they couldn't go to the hospital or call on a doctor. All they could do was get through the night in their dark, cramped room next to the house gate. Their little sister, now changed into the clothes their cousin's family had given them, was silent, not whimpering or groaning but instead barely *breathing. My mum, lying beside her, bit her own finger to draw blood. Reasoning that her baby sister might live if she drank her blood to make up for losing so much. The little one had lost a front tooth not long before, and my mum said her index finger fitted snugly in the little gap where a new tooth was budding. Said she liked how her blood flowed in through there. How she felt her sister suck the tip of her finger at one point, like an infant, and how, for a brief moment, she was so overjoyed she could barely breathe.*

Soot and flames smoulder inside Inseon's pupils. She shuts her eyes as if trying to stamp them out. When she opens her eyes again, the fire in them is no longer burning.

As her mind grew cloudier, the thing my mother talked about the most was what happened that night, she says.

The candle in my hand illuminates Inseon's face from below, and a dark shadow spreads over the bridge of her nose and her eyelids.

At the time, my mum was as strong as an ox. The whole time she was telling me this story, and even after she was done, she wouldn't let go of my hands. Until my wrists ached and I wanted to tug them free of her grip. She told me how every time she cut her finger and drew blood, she remembered. Every time she clipped a fingernail too short and nicked the skin, every time salt touched the still-healing wound, she remembered: the mouth sucking on her finger in the dark.

⌣

She had so many questions, my mum.

What do you think the little one was thinking as she crawled home? What made her crawl all that way, from that dark barley field where her umung and abang lay dead beside her, if not the thought of her sisters, that they would come back from their errand? That they could save her?

⌣

Inseon stops talking.

There's a noise in the other room.

A hushed sound you have to stifle your breath to hear. Like sand sifting in water, like rice grains being moved around by hand, the sound grows fractionally in volume before quietening down again.

Let's stay here, Inseon says softly, as if to stop me, though I haven't said anything.

They'll be fine without us, she goes on, whispering. They're not here to see us.

The sound of scattering rice grains and sifting sand slowly grows louder. We hear the rustle of feathers, the flap of wings and then, almost in chorus, low chirrups from the birdcage, the table, the kitchen sink. Are the birds here? I wonder. Not their shadows, but the actual birds, who flex their wing muscles to glide, who swing from the shaded lamp above the dining table.

We don't speak until the sounds have died down. The reverberations fade, a slowing eddy. Gradually, like a final cadence releasing into the air, like a face that, mid-whisper, falls into slumber, everything goes still.

5

Descent

I stare up at the darkened window. *It's like the hush underwater.* I imagine opening the window to a torrent of black water.

I once saw video footage transmitted from a camera mounted on an autonomous underwater vehicle as it sank into the deep sea. The dark green light refracting down from the surface grew faint, then was swallowed up in the murk. On the black screen, sporadic points of radiance appeared like ghosts and briefly shimmered: flashes emitted by distant ocean creatures. Occasionally these bioluminescent organisms came into full view on camera, only to plunge back into obscurity. The vertical stretch of sea where the points of light gleamed grew increasingly short. The solid opaque expanse that intersected with it grew overwhelmingly vast. After a while

I wondered if the dark was all that remained, but then the camera captured the translucent glow of a giant phantom jellyfish amid what looked like a heavy snowstorm. This white sediment was the skeletal remains of marine organisms, falling as ocean ooze. The light on the vehicle fizzled out from the water pressure. It was unclear whether the black of the last scene was in fact the abyss or simply a failed image transmission.

～

I didn't really know my mum as it turns out, Inseon says as she gets to her feet and heads over to the dark bookcase. And all the while I'd thought I knew her too well.

Her shadow lengthens past the ceiling, making her willowy body look even taller. She stands on tiptoe and reaches for a box on a higher shelf. I glimpse the skin of her lower calf over her short socks and bony ankles. Just as I'm wondering if I should offer to help, she catches the box against her chest.

～

Inseon sets the box down next to the map and rolls her sleeves a little higher before opening its lid. What could warrant such care?

The first thing she pulls out are scraps of discoloured newspaper clippings. A bundle of them, round which someone has wound cotton twine tied into a bow. Another bundle, this time of photographs layered with protective vellum paper, is the next to be placed on the map.

Inseon undoes the knot of the greyed twine round the clippings. The thread must have been white, seeing as there are pale flecks visible on the underside of the knot. The first clipping has the date 1960.7.28. and the name of the newspaper, E— Ilbo, written in blue biro ink in the margins, but not in Inseon's hand. These are in a neat hand that begins each vertical stroke with a sharp bend and has applied enough pressure to leave an imprint on the paper.

Oh no, Inseon groans. She has gently unfolded a clipping, only for the crumbling paper edge to fall away. She turns the clipping towards me. To read it, I'll have to get down on the floor and lean as close to the page as I can. The candlelight is too dim and the paper has darkened with time, so the only way to make out the figures in the image is by holding the candle right above it.

Before I kneel and lean forward as in a deep bow, I ask myself whether this is something I want to see, whether this isn't in the same category as the photos I saw by the wall of the hospital entrance: something best not looked at directly.

⁓

And still I get down on my knees. Moving the candle in sync with my eyes, I scan the crowd of hundreds gathered in a square in the black-and-white press photo. Most people seem to be dressed in bright, presumably white clothes. The brightness extends to the flags some are carrying. There's a banner hanging in the direction the crowd is facing, and I am able to read the Hanja calligraphy on it: Joint Memorial Rites for the Massacre Victims of Gyeongbuk Province. The article headline has the same Hanja for memorial rites, 慰靈祭, beneath which the same hand that recorded the date has written out the sounds for the three characters, wi-ryeong-je, and underlined passages in the article with the same firm pressure.

about 10,000 National Bodo League members from the Gyeongbuk region

1,500 inmates of Daegu Penitentiary

at the Gyeongsan Cobalt Mine and nearby Gachanggol

to excavate and recover remains from these sites of massacre

I realize the movement of my finger and eyes over the vertical writing more or less matches the pace at which I usually read out or silently mouth the words of a text. This might explain the presence I detect emanating from the text, like the faintest of voices. I read another passage that has been underscored heavily, which turns out to be part of a quote from a statement made by the association of the victims' families.

we have commissioned, in the spirit of the April 19th Revolution, a fact-finding group for the victims and the massacred

we ask the families of the victims to overcome their outdated fears and actively cooperate with our association's investigative efforts

‿

I'm confused. This E— Ilbo article is fifty-eight years old. Who could have made the clipping and marked up these passages?

I found it in a drawer of my mum's closet, Inseon tells me as I raise my bowed head. She wrote the way she'd been taught in school. Always with that forty-five-degree bend to her long strokes.

‿

Inseon reaches out a hand, and this time I don't mistake the gesture. She wants the candle.

As she gets up with the candle in one hand, I see the expression on her face. It isn't exhaustion, or magnanimity, or resignation. It reminds me of the look she had on her face that day years ago as she ladled hot juk into a bowl and said, *You know the saying – a good appetite, a long life. My mum's going to live a good long life.*

⌣

Inseon removes a thin box made out of woven bamboo from the collection of mostly paper boxes of a similar quality, albeit of varying sizes and states of wear. I take the candle from her once she returns and hold it up as she opens the lid and removes a flat parcel wrapped in dark red silk.

The silk wrapping reveals a faded envelope. Addressed in Hanja and in vertical writing to 姜正心. The commemorative stamp shows a man and a woman holding up the Korean flag and shouting 'manse' as they celebrate liberation. It is postmarked Daegu Post Office, 1950.5.4. Inseon removes the letter, written on coarse grey paper and folded twice, from the envelope. She hands it to me. A bluish-purple 'Censored' stamp is smudged across the upper left side of the paper. I bring the flame closer and read the first two lines of the letter, which is written top to bottom and from right to left:

Han Kang

J   T
e   o
         o
n   m
g   y
         s
i   s
m   i
         s
         t
         e
         r

The handwriting is tiny and the characters are a bit too spaced out. Maybe this says something about the writer, their personality.

I'm well, there's really no need for you to worry, he writes. Please send my regards to Jeongsook and Grandmother and the other elders, he writes. I have six years still to serve, but considering how many folk from Jeju were sentenced to fifteen and even seventeen years, I'm one of the lucky ones, he writes. I was so happy you wrote to me, I hope you'll write back again, he writes. Then, in characters the size of sesame seeds, he has added a *PS* and addressed something in an

296

earlier letter he received, which presumably had not sat right with him: *I read your letter and reflected a lot When I get out you will be twenty-one Jeongsook will be twenty-five and I'll be twenty-eight Of course I miss you but that's no reason to shed tears Not when we'll have so many more days together as many as the hairs on a cow to reminisce about the old days Please tell Jeongsook I said this*

Hanjinae was burned to the ground. There was nowhere left to return to, Inseon tells me as I hand back the letter. So my mum and aunt wound up staying with their grandmother and uncle and his wife at the distant cousin's place.

My mum told me that once the adults were asleep in a row on the floor of that tiny room, her sister would whisper in her ear that their brother would have made it out alive. He was always quick on his feet, she'd remind her. He'll have managed not to get caught. He'll know all the good hiding spots too; he's been helping Father herd horses in the hills since he was in middle school, she'd say. Remember how he would bring back wild berries in his empty lunch box afterwards to give to you and Jeongok? So he won't starve either, she'd say.

Inseon folds the letter back along its creases.

My mum told me that her baby sister cried over that lunch box once, she continues. My grandfather and uncle always brought a dosirak with them when they went herding, and that day she'd asked to eat their food and got a tongue-lashing from her mother. That night, my uncle came back and handed the nickel-silver box to my mum. Annoyed, thinking he was foisting the dishwashing on her, she opened the lid to find that he'd layered the box with leaves and nestled berries of all hues in them like jewels. *I thought you might share that with Jeongok*, he said with what my mum described as a bashful smile.

While Inseon takes a breath, I recall the wild mulberries from last autumn. How Inseon kept them in an air-tight container in her workshop. How my tongue and front teeth had turned dark purple when I drank the sour tea she made from simmering them.

On days when American reconnaissance planes dropped a blizzard of propaganda leaflets, leaflets that said anyone who turned themself in wouldn't be punished, my aunt would whisper to my mum that he might give himself up after reading the message. That since he was slight and looked younger than his age, he probably wouldn't be shot on his way down from the woods. That he was after all the most quick-witted and charming of the siblings and bound to get away by acting a bit clueless.

⁓

I see the winter light at the library again. That day six years ago, I'd resolutely walked past the records of oral histories from villages across this island, selected two other books and found a seat at a small desk at the end of an aisle. And from there had watched the light slide its way in through the blind slats. All afternoon, I read about how from mid November of 1948, the uplands of Jeju burned for three months and upwards of thirty thousand civilians were slaughtered. By the spring of 1949, when the scorched-earth policy was temporarily abandoned after the state failed to find the whereabouts of the roughly one hundred guerrillas, an estimated twenty thousand civilians were hiding out in Hallasan, mostly with their kin. They had judged it safer to brave starvation and the cold than risk facing summary executions along the shores. The commander who had been appointed to the island in March announced plans to sweep through Hallasan to eradicate all commie guerrillas and leaflet-bombed the island to flush civilians out to the coast for the efficiency of their operations. Archive photos showed rows of emaciated men and women walking down slopes, shielding children and elders with their bodies even as they held up branches tied with white cloth, an entreaty to the soldiers not to shoot.

~

But of course they reneged on their promise and rounded up people by the thousands. A relative was by some stroke of luck released and came to see them at the cousin's. He said some people were locked up in the dozen or so sweet-potato storehouses behind the alcohol plant and that he himself had been held there for two months, along with my uncle. That night my mum and aunt couldn't sleep from relief and happiness. At least they knew now that he wasn't dead.

Then the two of them went to the factory on the day and time the relative had jotted down for them.

They waited round a bend on the hillside behind the storehouses, in the spot he had marked out on the roughly drawn map, and eventually eight youths came up the slope. They were carrying water pails, and the last person in the row was my uncle. He looked even smaller after weeks of hunger, his hair was dull and matted, the mischievous twinkle in his eyes was gone, and my mum was struck by his unfamiliarity.

They embraced him from either side, but instead of wrapping his arms around them, he simply stood there, looking dazed. One of the men, who had a white armband and seemed to be guiding the way, said to him, I won't say anything; you talk while we get the water. It only took them ten minutes to come back with the water, and in that short span my mum said something she would regret for years to come.

What have you done to your hair, Oppa? It looks funny.

As soon as he graduated from middle school, my uncle had grown out his hair. He used to plant himself in front of a mirror every morning and carefully part his hair to one side, and slick it down with pomade. My mum would ask him if he was off to meet someone, and he'd dab a bit of grease right by the parting in her bobbed hair and tease her with mock deference, Is that what you do, Samchun, comb your hair only when you've people to see? He used to tell her about his plan to get a teaching certificate from the temporary teacher-training centre they'd set up in town — Keep this to yourself though, he'd insist. I'll tell Umung and Abang when I pass the exam — and sometimes when she asked him how many strokes a Hanja character had as she did her homework, he would show her how to use a Hanja dictionary and say, You should think about going to the centre too. There are women teachers in some of the town schools now, you know. Of course you'll first have to go to middle school.

But on this day he seemed so indifferent to every-thing, like a stranger. In a dull, empty voice, he asked if their parents and their youngest sibling were alive, then stared into my aunt's eyes as she answered truthfully. As if there was something beyond her face, something he might see if he could see past her eyes. He bolted down the rice balls she'd brought, then catching sight of the returning men, rushed towards them to take back his pail without so much as a look back at his sisters.

Exactly one week later, on the day they were to visit him again, my great-grandmother sold her ring to buy some rice and other groceries. She had barely eaten or stirred from bed since losing her only daughter, but now she was back up on her feet. She filled a nickel-silver dosirak with steamed rice, and two others with eggs cooked in a steamer, a whole fried fish, and some pork she'd stir-fried with potatoes and onions.

This time round he didn't look as dazed, which was something. He called them by their names and pointed at his hair, which he'd run his hands through with water, and asked my mum, How's my hair? It's not so funny now, is it?

My mum told me how good it felt to hear him say this. That day they sat down together on a rock and managed to eat nearly half the food the sisters had brought. They laughed together too, she said. And held hands before saying goodbye.

The following week, the sisters went back and waited in the same spot, but this time no one showed up. When they'd waited close to an hour, a woman living nearby shouted over her wall, They shipped them out overnight, the folk in the storehouses.

My aunt told my mum they couldn't leave on a stranger's word alone. What if they missed him altogether? She insisted they should wait for him until dark. My mum would doze, or pet and tickle the dog that came to sniff at the food, but she said her sister never took her eyes off that bend in the road.

✦

I close my eyes.

I see it again. The light stealing past the slats over the west-facing window in increasingly wide swathes to eventually reach my face where I sat in the library aisle. I'd imagined, in the radiance of that light, that the blood running beneath the numbers I'd encountered on the page might simply evaporate. I eventually moved to a seat where the sun wasn't directly in my eyes, but I remember to this day the tangible sensation I had that the footnote I was reading, even as it testified to events that took place in the depths of night, was emitting its own light:

After nearly twelve hours on the night boat, we arrived at Mokpo, but they wouldn't let us off the ship until it was night again. I was famished and dehydrated and barely managed to disembark. It was drizzling and I remember the pontoon was slippery. The dock quickly filled up with over a thousand people, and hundreds of cops with guns made us line up, women with women, men with men. Anyone under eighteen was placed in a separate group. It took a long while to get everyone sorted. It was summer, but it had rained all night and plenty of folk were coughing, or they stumbled or sank to the ground. We were told to climb into a convoy of police cars, and I heard a young woman in the back wail, No, no! She had a baby that must have died on the way over, from hunger or disease, I don't know, and the cops had told her to leave the baby behind. She was writhing in protest, but two cops grabbed the baby by its swaddling cloth, set it on the ground, then dragged the woman to the front and into one of the cars.

It's the strangest thing, but more than the unspeakable torture I experienced . . . more than the years I spent locked up without cause, it's that woman's voice that still haunts me. And the more than one thousand folk who, as they shuffled ahead in their rows, kept looking back at that abandoned bundle on the dock.

I open my eyes and look at Inseon.
   Descending.

Past the reach of the light from the water surface.
Past the point where gravity overtakes buoyancy.

I found this in the sewing box, Inseon says, placing the letter back in its silk wrapping. My mum had sewn it into the lining of the lid. If she hadn't told me to get it for her, I'd never have found it.

I realize why the darkened red fabric seemed familiar. It's the same quilted silk enveloping the tin lid of the sewing box. Perhaps that was her own way of camouflaging what she wanted to hide? Would she have removed the seam and sewn it back each time she read the letter?

The first time a letter from my uncle was delivered to the cousin's home was in March 1950, Inseon tells me. My mum wrote back, and this was the answer she received in May. She kept this letter, but she doesn't have the first one, as my aunt took that with her.

I knew a few vague details about Inseon's aunt. That she had lived in Seoul, that she had been taller and had a louder voice than Inseon's mum, that she'd had handsome features. During the summer breaks she would visit Jeju with her granddaughter and stay for as long as a month. She doted on her niece, who was younger than her granddaughter, and used to send winter scarves and gloves she'd knitted for the little girl. She'd passed away at an early age from an illness around the time Inseon entered middle school.

Soon after that first letter came, my aunt got married by arrangement. Inseon knits her brows together into a familiar frown. It's inconceivable to me how they could entertain the idea of marriage in all that chaos, but my mum said the Seocheong were above and beyond the law and terrorized the islanders in unimaginable ways. Rapes, kidnappings and murders had become so commonplace that anyone with young daughters was anxious to have them married off as soon as they found a decent match. This postscript, where he asks my mum to tell Jeongsook not to cry, was his answer to what my mum wrote in her letter about my aunt, how she'd stayed up all night before her wedding, fretting and in fear for him.

Inseon places the bundle of letters on the floor by her knees, then lays a palm over it. The careful gesture suggests something might wriggle its way out from under the silk.

The following month war broke out, and the letters stopped coming.

Inseon's voice is low.

But my mum wasn't worried. The adults told her he would be fine as Daegu Penitentiary was below the Nakdong River front.

Inseon's palm lifts from the letters and settles over her lap.

Like most Jeju men, my aunt's husband joined the navy when the war began. My mum and aunt lived in fear until he returned unharmed, three years later. The lockdown order on Hallasan was lifted around then too, and after all that time living at the cousin's, the adults could finally build a new home. My mum helped stack stones and carry logs too. After all that effort though, they barely lived a year in this place. After the armistice, a relative who had settled in Seoul and was making a living selling American army surplus goods suggested a partnership to my great-uncle. As my aunt's husband had been wanting to get away from Jeju, he and my aunt went with him, while Mum chose to remain here and care for my great-grandmother.

⌣

Before the sisters went their separate ways, they made a trip to Daegu Penitentiary in May of 1954.

Inseon's calm voice speaks into the stillness.

Mum was nineteen, my aunt twenty-three that year.

⌣

But they didn't find my uncle there.

There was only a record that said four years earlier, in July, he had been transferred to Jinju. There was no direct transport to Jinju, so the sisters headed for Busan. They stayed a night at an inn by the train station, set off for Jinju as soon as the sun came up, and caught a bus to the local prison.

My uncle wasn't there either. There was no record

of his transfer, not in Jinju. The next day, they went to Yeosu, to the port. My aunt insisted she wouldn't head to Seoul until she'd seen my mum off first. So they waited for the ship that would take my mum to Jeju, and that was when my aunt said, Let's give up. He's dead. The day of his transfer, we'll consider that the day he died.

⁓

Inseon slips her hands inside the box that had stored the brittle clippings. It seems she is able to find what she needs by touch alone, because in no time she is handing me a sheaf of papers that have been stapled together.

A stack of A4 sheets that feel smooth to the touch, perhaps from their fluorescent coating, and that seem to have bypassed time. They're photocopies of a handwritten list of names and serial numbers. Above the hundreds of names, all written in vertical text, a date stamp marks a day in July 1949. The stamps in the remarks column down the page, however, are different, and vary between 9, 27 and 28 July of 1950. On the third page, right at the top, a vertical line has been drawn in pencil beside one name.

姜
正
勳

Beneath the remarks column under the name Kang Jeonghun, I see two stamp marks: '1950.7.9' and 'Transferred to Jinju'. What's odd is how beneath each of the more than thirty 'Transferred to Jinju' stamps on the list, I can see something else written by hand. I can't immediately make out what it says, but by piecing together the strokes of the same repeating comment that are visible below the ink, I eventually read: *Handed over to army/police.*

Where did you get this? I ask.

I didn't get it.

Then who did? I'm about to say when the answer dawns on me. It can't have been easy to come by copies of documents like this one. I recall the light, wrinkled hands, reaching towards my own from under a blanket. I hear the voice saying, Enjoy your visit. I remember the suspicion, the caution, the muted warmth of her eyes as they looked into mine.

⌒

The number of Bodo League members in Gyeongbuk alone who died that year is about ten thousand. And, as I'm sure you know, they estimate that at least a hundred thousand people died nationwide.

I nod, even as I turn these words over in my mouth: *They killed a lot more than that, didn't they?*

I knew about the organization, how back in 1948, after the first government was established, whole swathes of people were categorized as left-wingers in need of education and made to join the League so that they might benefit from its purported goal to convert, protect and guide. If someone in your family had ever been in the audience of a political talk, you had to join. The government had set quotas, and many people were enrolled by village and neighbourhood heads intent on meeting those quotas, or signed up voluntarily after hearing about the rice and fertilizers they would receive. Entire families were enrolled as well, meaning its 'members' included women, children and the elderly, and when war broke out in the summer of 1950, everyone on the list was preventively detained, then summarily executed. The estimated number of people killed and buried in secret around the country is said to be between two hundred thousand and three hundred thousand.

⌒

That summer, any Bodo League member who was detained in Daegu was held at Daegu Penitentiary, Inseon says. The vellum paper rustles as she picks up the bundle of photographs.

Each day hundreds more arrived in trucks and soon they ran out of space to hold them all and began picking out earlier inmates to shoot dead. Of the roughly one and a half thousand political prisoners who died then, one hundred and forty were from Jeju.

Inseon loosens the twine and removes the paper to reveal a grainy black-and-white photo of skulls in the foreground.

This is the cobalt mine in Gyeongsan. It was abandoned by the Japanese in 1945 and stood empty at the time.

The focus is off, but it's still possible to make out the empty eye sockets and nasal cavities particular to human skulls. Behind them crouch three middle-aged men. They are in light, untucked short-sleeved shirts, holding torches. From the sharp angle of the photo, I can guess that the ceiling must have been very low.

Around three and a half thousand people were killed here. Inmates of Daegu Penitentiary, members of Daegu Bodo League, and even members from Gyeongbuk who had been held in warehouses near the Gyeongsan Police Headquarters.

Inseon reaches for the list of names in my hand.

Over many days, military trucks drove in and out of the mine. There are accounts from residents of how the sound of gunfire continued from early dawn to the middle of the night. When the drifts and shaft were full of corpses, they simply moved into the hills and went on killing and burying in a nearby valley.

She places a finger on the pencil mark drawn beside the name Kang Jeonghun.

This stamp is dated 9 July, meaning my uncle was probably killed in the mine and not in the valley. The people whose names are dated 28 July are likely to have died in the valley, and as for those taken away on 27 July, there's no way to tell at which of the two sites their remains may be found.

～

I stare at the line Inseon was pointing to a moment ago. A firm line, if not quite as forceful as the blue biro line. I rub it with my fingertip and feel the fine indentation against my skin. Did the person who drew this line also know? Did she figure out the relationship between the handover dates and the site of execution, as Inseon has just outlined for me?

～

The summer of 1960 was when the families of those murdered here first came to see the mine, Inseon says. After the wartime authorities stepped down following the April 19th Revolution.

Inseon carefully leafs through the disintegrating articles until she comes to a clipping folded in half. She opens it and I see the entire social issues section minus a lower strip where an ad would have been. It's the same publication the clipping about the memorial rites was taken from. This article predates the memorial by roughly one month.

They reported on how the victims' families were visiting the mine for the first time, ten years later, Inseon explained. The families took this picture at the time, but no outlet would print it, so they each held on to a copy, hoping they would one day get it published.

Sure enough, the article doesn't show any images from inside the mine. Next to the lead story is a single wide-shot photo of the entrance to the mine. To the left of this picture, there's an interview with the representative of the association of the victims' families.

After ten years of exposure to water flowing through the mine and general decomposition, the remains were all scattered. In short, there wasn't a single set of remains left intact. We visited without much forethought or equipment and there weren't enough of us to recover the remains, so we took one photo and came back up. Our own estimates put the number of dead at 3,000 minimum, and in the first horizontal drift, which is what I've seen so far, there were some 500 or 600 sets of remains.

There's concrete blocking the vertical shaft at the moment, so we'll have to blast through that before we can access the lower drift and determine the full extent of what took place.

The sentences are composed, calm, though in life they would have borne the inflections of a Gyeong-buk dialect. I sense something oozing from the page, something viscous that trickles out caked and thick like red-bean juk, and blood-metallic, following the candle's trajectory.

How did she manage to find these articles? I ask Inseon. I doubt a Gyeongbuk paper would have been distributed in Jeju.

She went and bought them herself, of course, Inseon says matter-of-factly. I realize that the person I should be picturing right now isn't the elderly woman who reached her wrinkled hands out to me, but the woman in the black-and-white photo who had looked back at the camera, her compact figure pulsing with life.

I think she must have attended the memorial in front of Daegu Station. There's a flyer from the event somewhere.

The article about the memorial by the station is still lying open. I move the candle and peer at the photo again. About two-thirds of the people in the crowd are women. Hundreds of women stand facing the banner in traditional mourning clothes, their waists bound tight, or in white knee-length dresses.

⌣

Was this how she would have dressed? I look closely at the blurred profiles of the women, their features indistinct and smudged. In the portrait I saw, had she been in a round-neck dress with short sleeves? I'm about to get up to retrieve the framed photo from the box, but Inseon reaches across the empty air towards me. I read the recipient's name written in navy-blue ink on the manila envelope she's holding out.

姜正心 貴下. Respectfully addressed to Kang Jeongsim.

There's a blue-purple rectangular stamp mark next to the sender's Daegu address. By the light of my candle, I read: The Association of Bereaved Families of the Massacred of Gyeongbuk.

I slide my hand inside the cold envelope. I remove a small booklet made from several sheets of coarse paper folded into eights and bound with staples. I turn the first page, which is also the cover, and find a letter on the next page.

Our anguished wishes are finally to be honoured, for after ten years of longing, we are to meet our beloveds and lay them to rest.

A lengthy, impassioned sentence that reminds me of the line 'we ask the families of the victims to overcome their outdated fears . . .' Maybe they were both written by the same person. I don't read further and turn the page to find a grainy black-and-white group photo.

They took this in front of the cobalt mine that winter in 1960, Inseon explains. I don't think my mum was there. But she got it in the mail as a fee-paying member of the bereaved families' association. Inseon points to a man in glasses standing in the middle of the group. This is the president of the association, she says. He was arrested the following year after the military coup in May and sentenced to death. The secretary, who's standing next to him, received a fifteen-year sentence.

On the next page is an even grainier copy of

the photo taken inside the mine, the one the families are said to have each held on to, with a caption beneath it. If I hadn't seen the image before, I doubt I could have told the figures apart, as all detail and any tonal range that falls between white and black have been lost in reproduction. Someone has left a clipping of a short article from the social issues section of a national evening paper between the pages.

～

The clipping has obviously been handled a lot, and the criss-crossing fold lines have worn away to white. Beneath the Hanja for 'sentenced to death', 死刑言渡, in blue ink, someone has noted the pronunciation for the most complicated of the four characters, 渡: 'do'. I can make out a Daegu phone number as well, written in the margins.

Isn't this number . . .

The same as this one. Inseon reaches out, riffles through the booklet and points to the bottom of the very last page. A Nonghyup account number and the account holder's name for membership fees and donations are printed alongside the same phone number with its Daegu area code.

⌒

The white paper cup in the palm of my left hand emits a subtle yet unmistakable heat. The coating inside reflects the candle's flame like a curved mirror. I look down as if into a brightly lit circular interior, and gather my thoughts.

In the summer of 1961, they wouldn't have had a landline here. To make a phone call, she would have had to head into town.

On the luminous curved surface of the cup, I see the woman walk the exact path I stumbled my way through in the night, but in the opposite direction. At the forked road where I lost my footing and fell down the dry stream bed, this other woman veers and strolls through lush summer trees until she reaches a road with a bus stop.

Was the twice-folded newspaper clipping in her pocket? Or did she have it tucked away in a bag or held tight in a clammy fist? Why did she write down the number of the association? Why try their office when its working members had already been imprisoned? Did she actually make the call? If she did, who would have answered?

⌣

My maternal great-grandmother passed away in February of 1960, Inseon says. My mum was twenty-five at the time. Well past her marrying age by the standards of the day, which made everyone worry, but my mum wasn't interested in getting married. Her family assured her that she could stay at home until she found a match, but she bought this house with the money she'd saved up and carried on farming, all by herself. Then, that summer, she began looking for his remains.

Inseon takes a breath.

She searched for about a year, until she came across this article.

⌣

Our eyes meet in the stillness.

Sinking deeper still.

*Past the zone where the pressure bears down like
thunder and living creatures no longer emit light.*

After that, the archive stops. There aren't any
more clippings, not for thirty-four years.

I repeat the words inside my mouth. *For
thirty-four years.*

. . . Not until the military junta loses power
and a civilian is elected president.

6

The Deep Sea

I had placed my hand over the clipping, its crease lines, out of an urge to touch the traces of the hands that had scribbled down the phone number. Inseon didn't move to stop me when I picked up the sheaf of brittle papers. Turning over a discoloured press cutting featuring a news-in-brief article about the 1961 Military Revolutionary Committee trials, I find another clipping that leaps ahead thirty-four years. The typesetting has changed from vertical right-to-left to horizontal left-to-right, and the headline contains only one or two Hanja words.

From this point on, I have my own memories of that time, Inseon says. One of those summers, I came down for a visit and saw that a national daily newspaper and a Gyeongbuk daily newspaper were being delivered to my mum. It took the national paper a couple of days and the local paper about three days to arrive in the mail. I had questions, but I didn't ask her about it. I thought someone must have encouraged her to subscribe or was sending her copies for free.

I hold the candle over the headline of the 1995 article. It reports that a citizen group from Gyeongsan has held the very first rites to console the dead in front of the cobalt mine. The next clipping is an article from 1998. Bereaved families from all across Gyeongbuk Province gathered outside the mine for a joint memorial ceremony. The cuttings from 1999 are mostly of editorials. They argue that however long after the fact it was now, the remains should be exhumed from the mine, and quickly, as the bereaved are getting older. In the top margins of all the clippings, the year and date are written in permanent marker and in pencil. The handwriting looks similar to the blue biro markings from 1960, but there is less pressure on the paper and the writing is nearly twice as large.

The first clipping from 2000 is from the front page of a newspaper, which features a colour photo taken of a group of elders gathered at the entrance to the mine. The article is about the association of the cobalt-mine victims' families reassembling after forty years. At this point, there's a surge in clippings. As we move into 2001, articles begin to announce an upcoming expedition into the lower drift of the mine jointly organized by a public broadcasting company, the citizen group from Gyeongsan and representatives of the associations of bereaved families. These are followed by photos from the survey team's entry as well as stills from a documentary programme that were pre-released before the programme aired.

With each turn of the crumbling newspaper clippings, more skeletal remains are revealed in the candlelight. Skulls photographed from one side, front views of empty eye sockets and the sunken spaces where noses would have been, femurs, tibias. There are remains whose shoulder blades, spines and pelvises jut out from the mine floor to loosely form a human figure.

I hold the candle over the reporter's account, which has been underlined in places with a pencil. The article says the survey team set off dynamite at the mouth of the vertical shaft that connects the surface to the horizontal drifts below. Once they blasted through the concrete that had sealed it off for fifty years, a staggering number of skeletal remains poured out of the shaft, so many that there was no room for the group to make any sort of descent. That entry point had been the site of the executions. The article says it was assumed that the victims had been made to stand at its edge, then were shot from behind and had fallen into the shaft. It appeared that after the lower drift filled with corpses, more bodies had piled up on top of those and into the upper drift, and that when the shaft itself was crammed with bodies up to the surface, the soldiers had decamped.

～

I set down the clippings.

I don't want to see any more bones. I don't want my fingerprints resting over those of the person who'd gathered these articles.

～

That was just a one-off undertaking, Inseon says, pushing herself up off the floor.

They didn't formally begin exhuming the remains until six years later.

She is feeling around the dark bottom shelf of the bookcase when her hands pause on something.

In three years, around four hundred sets of

remains were recovered before they halted the exhumations in 2009. Meaning more than three thousand people's remains are still down there.

She pulls out a large book that looks to be about a thousand pages.

Those three years, 2007 to 2009, were also when remains were exhumed from mass graves throughout the country.

She sets the book on the floor and slowly pushes it towards me. I glance at the cover. It is a collection of data that was published when excavation efforts nationwide tentatively came to a stop.

And it was during those years, Inseon says, that I saw the newspaper photo of the bones beneath the runway.

⁓

I don't want to open it. I'm not the least bit curious. No one can force me to wade through those pages. I am under no obligation to comply.

But my trembling hands reach out and open the book. I turn page after page of photographs showing skeletal remains that have been separated and sorted into huge plastic baskets: thousands of shin bones. Thousands of skulls. Tens of thousands of ribs. Then more photos: hundreds of wooden name stamps, belt buckles, school uniform buttons engraved with the character 中 meaning 'middle', silver hairpins of varied lengths and widths, playing marbles that resemble glass beads with wings inside – all scattered over four hundred pages of the book.

~

In the end, my mum failed.

Inseon's voice has grown so quiet, I feel as if she's somewhere far away.

She never recovered his bones. Not a single one.

How much further into these depths can we go? Is this the silence that lies below the ocean in my dream?

Beneath the tidal waves that rose up to my knees.

Leagues below the hollowed-out graves dotting the plain.

~

Not even two sweaters and two coats can block out the cold I'm feeling. It is a chill that seems to have originated not from outside but from within my chest. I can't stop shivering, and as everything in the room begins to undulate in the unsteady shadows cast by the candlelight, I understand why Inseon denied any intentions of making a film about these events.

The smell of blood-soaked clothes and flesh rotting together, the phosphorescence of bones that have been decaying for decades will be erased. Nightmares will slip through fingers. Excessive violence will be removed. Like what was omitted from the book I wrote four years ago. The flame-throwers that soldiers deployed on unarmed citizens in the streets. The people rushed to emergency rooms on improvised stretchers, burn blisters on their faces, their bodies doused in white paint from head to toe to prevent identification.

I raise my body up off the ground.

Inseon's faint shadow passes straight through the flame to rest over the pale wall by the bookcase. It flits away as I approach. I run my fingers over the faded wallpaper and lay a hand over the spot where her face was. As if the firmness of this cool wall might yield to me the secrets of this strange night. As if there are questions I can only ask the vanished shadow, not Inseon, who watches me silently from behind.

⁓

I used to think my mum was the weakest person I knew.

Inseon's hoarse voice traces a line through the stillness.

A phantom.
    I thought of her as a living ghost.

I leave the book open on the floor and head towards the dark window. I hold the candle closer and turn to face Inseon.

What I didn't know was that during those three years, the Jeju branch of the bereaved families' association for the missing Daegu prisoners had been regularly visiting that mine.

And that my mum had been one of the regular visitors.

She was in her early seventies then, and those three years were also when the arthritis in her knees got increasingly worse.

With each step I take, the flame's shadows make the whole room sway. Even after I've crossed the room again and taken a seat opposite Inseon, the lurching does not stop as my breath too is still coming out in shudders from the chill.

⌣

It was in the spring, the year before last, when I found the contact information for the president of the Jeju bereaved families' association and met up with him in town.

He was a retired high-school teacher born the month the war broke out, who had never known his father, yet decades after hadn't given up on finding his father's remains.

He apologized for not having offered his condolences sooner, as he hadn't heard the news of my mother's passing until later. He told me she had been the most passionate member of the association, that she had already been to Gyeongsan in 1960 when no one else in Jeju would have even thought to go there. It had also been her idea to request a copy of the list of inmates at Daegu Penitentiary who'd been transferred to Jinju. Only after they had chartered a van and visited the penitentiary together to protest did they receive the list, and my mum was the one who went through it page by page and not only found the names of the other members' missing relatives but told them where their remains were likely to be buried. She was always the first one to leave when they met downtown as she lived the furthest away, and every time, as she said goodbye, she would hold the hands of each member in her palms.

The last memory the president had of her was from the day they learned exhumation was to be halted, when they'd gone into the mine all together. The secretary of the Gyeongsan association held up a torch and guided them inside — the roof was low, and two runnels of water were flowing over the ground, so everyone wore helmets and rubber boots that came up to their knees. When they stooped to pass through an untouched section where bones and mouldered scraps of clothes peeked up through the dirt, everyone — all of them elderly — held on to each other so they wouldn't fall. And my mum used her free hand, the one that wasn't gripping her walking cane, to grab this man's sleeve, smiling gently.

Sorry, I'll need to trouble you for a second, she said.

The president helped my mum back through the drift and, once they made it out, they started exchanging greetings with the other members.

Before they all parted ways though, the secretary said, There are rumours that there were three survivors at the time, but I think it's more likely there was only one. Isn't it fair to assume that the same person will have knocked on the doors of three nearby homes?

At his mention of 'survivors', the whole group had fallen silent.

The secretary continued: I heard that it was a clear night with a half-moon and not a single cloud in the sky. A baby-faced young man in bloodstained clothes asked for clean ones to change into, swearing not to tell anyone where he'd got them. The times being what they were, two houses refused him, but one took the risk. They say he changed into the clean

*clothes right there in the yard, then ran off, quick as
a bolt.*

*The president said his heart tensed hearing that
story. He was listening intently so as not to miss a
single word, and when he finally remembered where
he was and looked around, he saw my mother squat-
ting over the ground, vomiting. She did not stop
until she was retching nothing but stomach acid.*

⌣

There's a not-zero chance that young man
could be my uncle, Inseon whispers. Just like
there's a chance my uncle could be any one of
the three thousand sets of remains still inside
that mine.

Of course, she adds, nodding as if she were
seeking assent, I would guess that if the man were
my uncle, he would have somehow found his
way back to the island in the years since . . . but
can I even be sure of that? After surviving that
hell, would he still have been the kind of person
who made choices we could understand?

⌣

That may have been when my mother began to experience a rift within herself.

The day her brother's fate on that night splintered in two.

As one body among thousands piled up inside that mine.

And as a young man knocking on gates. Swearing not to tell a soul who had given him the new clothes. Please burn these, right away. *A young man who left his bloodied prison uniform in the yard and took off running, disappearing into the night.*

◡

I'm not convinced.

I only question how he could have survived.

By passing out and falling down the mineshaft, thus narrowly avoiding the bullet? By opening his eyes amid the heaps of corpses once the soldiers left? By crawling his way to the mouth of the upper drift by the light of the moon?

◡

I see the man creeping along the drift, see his eyes, then I see Inseon's overlay them. How did he make it back? I ask.

Inseon directs her eyes, which are so much like those of the man with the porcelain features and gleam sharp and bright as though they are always wet with tears, straight at me.

Who are you talking about?

I gently push aside my concern that what I say may harm the other person, and answer.

. . . Your father.

She isn't hurt.

She's stronger than I thought.

Without hesitation, without lowering her voice, she tells me, That was why my mum went looking for my father. To ask him how he'd made it out alive.

⌒

She said it was summer when the two of them first met.

For over a year, my mum had heard the rumours about someone who had returned to the island after serving a fifteen-year sentence in Daegu. She had seen glimpses of him from afar as he was staying at a relative's house in the lower village, but she said she needed more time to pluck up the courage to meet with him.

My father was enduring each day of the silent shunning.

He had hand tremors from being tortured, but it wasn't so bad that he couldn't pitch in and harvest mandarins with his relatives as thanks for their putting him up. He'd also learned to lay tiles during his last years in prison and put that skill to use doing odd jobs around the village for no pay, slowly building up a reputation for it. But under the military regime, no one would dream of being seen chit-chatting with an ex-con whom the police checked in on twice a month.

One summer evening, my mum stood waiting on the street corner until she saw him and called out, Samchun. My father turned round in surprise that anyone there would be addressing him with such warmth. My mum said his eyes changed when she told him my uncle's name. He had recognized her as one of the Hanjinae siblings who used to visit his maternal relatives.

But he had no wish to speak to her. Even in late autumn, when she went to see him again, he politely turned her away. It was only in the new year, when she went to see him in early spring, that he finally agreed to talk. He was afraid of people's watchful eyes, so he told her they should meet somewhere in town.

The following Sunday afternoon, when they sat across from each other in a tea room choked with cigarette smoke, my mother was thirty and my father thirty-six.

The first thing my mother learned that day was that my father had been transferred to another prison in Busan in the spring of 1950. The Daegu High Court presided over appellate cases not only within Gyeongsang Province but also from Jeolla Province and Jeju, so as more judgments were made, the number of inmates at Daegu Penitentiary continued to climb until the place grew too crowded to hold them. My father said the reason for the mass transfer of long-term prisoners that spring was as simple and pragmatic as that. He was one of the unlucky ones from Jeju with a longer sentence, but this was what saved him in the end.

Busan hadn't been safe either, though, he said.

Starting in July, Bodo League members from Busan were being herded into the penitentiary there. A temporary building had to be put up in the prison yard, and it was the inmates who were tasked with the labour. During breaks, my father would look across the yard at the tents set up round its perimeter and see half-naked children lethargic with hunger, women with their hair plaited or pulled back into low buns, and elders who kept their traditional hats on despite the scorching summer heat, all of them sweating profusely as they sat packed together in tight row upon row.

When September came and they began trucking those people away, panicked rumours started going around. Whispers that political prisoners would be weeded out and killed. And, sure enough, ninety or so of the two hundred and fifty people from Jeju were soon taken away. The remaining islanders were anxiously waiting to see who would be next when the summonses suddenly stopped. He later learned that the Allied Forces had landed in Incheon, changing the course of the war.

Did he hide his hands in his pockets, worried about knocking over his glass of water? I wonder.

Or did he keep them out, placed squarely on the table for all to see?

～

Then my father spoke about the very thing my mum had hoped to learn.

Whether the two of them had ever met, my uncle and my father, during the eight months or so between the summer my uncle was incarcerated at Daegu and the spring my father was transferred to Busan, when their sentences overlapped. And what my father remembered about him, if they did.

My father told her the arrival of three hundred people from Jeju that summer was a welcome occasion — more than anything, it was a chance to hear news about family back home. That was when my father learned that the people from Secheon who were rounded up and taken to the elementary school in P— had been shot dead on the beach. The man who told him about this also mentioned my uncle. He'd come over by boat with a young man whose mother's side of the family was from Secheon-ri and who ended up placed in the neighbouring cell block. Hearing his name alone, my father knew right away

*who he was. They had never gone to school together,
but he still remembered how, when they were younger,
the other boy and his younger siblings would sometimes come over to his side of the stream to play.
Maybe because they were both sons from families
with many daughters, they got along well and liked
to play with their sisters, mashing balsam flowers
with stones and staining their siblings' and their own
fingernails with the dye.*

But that was all.

*There was nothing more my father could tell the
woman seated across from him.*

⁓

*I asked my mum on several occasions about their
relationship after that day. Five more years passed
from that first meeting before my father came to live
in this house, and I was curious about their inter-
actions. How often they had seen each other. When
they grew closer. She never gave me a straight
answer. Instead, she told me random stories. She
would recount what my father had told her about the
torture he'd endured at the alcohol factory. How a
man in a military uniform with no insignia who
spoke the northern dialect had treated him. What the*

man said each time he stripped my father and tied him upside down to a chair.

We'll slaughter every last one of you commie sons of bitches, wipe you clean off the face of the earth. We'll stamp the life out of you rats if there's even a drop of red in you.

The man dumped bucket after bucket of water on my father's head, around which he'd tied a towel. He wrapped field telephone wires round my father's sopping wet chest and ran the electricity. Each time he whispered for my father to give up the names of his friends who'd been in secret contact with the people hiding in the hills, my father answered: I don't know. I'm innocent. I've done nothing wrong.

When she'd finished telling this story, my mum would start berating herself for something else, something I didn't understand.

Why did I have to comment on his hair that day? Was that all I could think to say?

She would let go of my hands as she said this. Her painful grip on me slackened like foam collapsing. It was like someone had blown a fuse within her. Like she'd forgotten who I was. Like she couldn't stand another human body touching hers, not for a second.

PART THREE

Flame

Do you feel that?

Inseon whispered as if she were trying to avoid straining.

Feel what? I said.

Just now. Didn't it get warmer? Just a bit?

Has it? I wondered. Has my breath stopped shuddering from the chill? Is there some type of vapour, or a distilled, diffuse gas swirling about and faintly lightening the air? A child opening her eyes in a dark barley field. *How's my hair? It's not so funny now, is it?* A baby in a windbreaker, curls sprouting from her head like tufts of grass.

In lieu of an answer, I placed my hand over the photo of the bones.

Over people who no longer had eyes or tongues.

Over people whose organs and muscles had rotted away.

Over what was no longer human – no.
Over what remained human even now.

In the suffocating stillness, I wondered: Is this it?
The brink of a gaping trench opening up below the abyssal plain,
the very bottom of the deep sea where nothing emits light?

⌒

Inseon held out her hand. She was asking for the candle.

She used its incandescence as a guide as she crossed the room and slid open the door, her shadow fluttering on the ceiling like a pair of wings. I got up too. I stepped over the sill and walked past the larger bedroom, noticed something faintly luminous like mercury pooled in front of the wardrobe and stopped short, sensing something dark as if steeped in meok crouched over it. But in the absence of more light I couldn't make out anything else.

Inseon had been continuing ahead on tiptoe but paused now and looked back at me.

Let's go and see it, she whispered, finger pressed to her lips.

See what?

Where we'll plant our trees, she said, nodding as if agreeing on my behalf. It's not far from here.

Now?

It won't take long.

But it's so dark out, I said. And there's not much of the candle left.

It's fine, Inseon said. We can come back before it runs out.

I stood still, hesitating. I didn't want to go there. But I didn't want to stay here in this stillness any more either.

Feeling the silence, taut as fabric in an embroidery hoop, and noticing how the sound of my own breath pierced that hush like a needle, I approached Inseon. She handed me the candle. While I held it, she bent down and put on her work shoes. When she stood again, I handed the candle back to her. And like sisters for whom this kind of wordless back-and-forth was second nature, she shone the light on me in turn as I laced up my trainers.

Before we stepped outside, I rummaged around the shelves of the shoe cabinet and grabbed the matches. I shook the box and heard maybe three or four matchsticks rattling around inside. I put the box in my coat pocket and stepped out into the yard. All I could see in the dark was the circle cast by the candle Inseon was carrying. The snowflakes falling from the sky winked in its glow for only as long as they passed through its perimeter, then disappeared.

Kyungha, Inseon called out. You step only where I've stepped, okay?

The light moved a little closer as Inseon held her arm out towards me.

Do you see my footprints?

I do, I said, pressing my feet into the little hollows she had made in the snow.

I kept two paces of distance between us so as not to run into Inseon or fall too far outside the radius I needed to see her footprints. We forged ahead, two bodies moving to the same choreography. The sound of snow crunching beneath our feet in tempo faded into the cold.

When we passed the tree under which Ama and Ami were buried, its drooping fronds entered the ring of light and came into sharp relief. Inseon pressed on, not sparing the tree so much as a glance. Her gait was unwavering, as though she believed the bird she had buried was long gone from there.

Inseon stopped before the wall at the edge of the yard. Once I caught up to her and took the candle, she gripped the stone surface with both hands and hoisted herself over. I handed the candle back to her and climbed up too. As soon as my feet had cleared the wall, Inseon resumed her trek.

$\smile$

I was planting my feet squarely inside the tracks Inseon had made, but I couldn't stop my trainers and the hems of my trousers from getting soaked. I kept walking, arms out for balance, focused on maintaining that two-pace interval. Whenever snowflakes landed on my eyelashes, I rubbed them away with the back of my hand. I wanted to know whether Inseon felt the same sudden chill as I did. Was this snow seeping into her cheeks too? If she was a spirit, how far did she plan to take me?

We entered a wooded area, though I couldn't identify the trees around us on account of the snow and dark. Inseon's footsteps made a gradual arc, as if there were a bend in the road. The light bobbed up and down, etching a red line in the air. Like an indecipherable railway signal. Like an immeasurably slow arrow in flight.

Inseon was starting to slow down. I tried to slacken my own pace to match hers. Not a breath of wind was blowing. The snowflakes brushing past my cheeks felt unbelievably soft. Two steps ahead of me, the flame in the paper cup was quivering in silence like a steady pulse.

Do we have much further to go?

We're almost there, Inseon answered without turning round.

I looked up at the blanketed trees. Their crowns were invisible. When the candle passed over the branches within view, the snow glittered like salt flakes.

Inseon-ah, I called.

I stopped short, breaking the rhythm of our strides. She kept walking, moving further away from me.

Inseon, wait.

She turned to me, face partly illuminated.

Her hands were stained a subtle red from the flame.

How much of the candle is left?

We're still fine.

I saw that only about a third of a finger's length of the pale stub remained at the bottom of the cup. We could turn back this instant and the wick would still be done before we made it to the house.

Once we're through these woods, we'll be at the stream, Inseon said reassuringly.

Impossible, I thought. We were heading a different way than I remembered. But it was possible that I'd lost my sense of direction. Maybe the stream ran a ring around the woods.

Let's go back, I said. Let's come out again later, once it's stopped snowing.

Inseon gave a stubborn shake of her head.

. . . There may not be a next time.

~

I stopped worrying about the candle.

I stopped keeping track of the distance to Inseon's house.

Just as I was beginning to feel like I didn't

want our walk to end, that I would gladly never turn back, Inseon looked round at me.

We're here, she said.

No trees were within range of the light in her hand. Utter darkness shrouded its glow. We were out of the woods.

I trailed Inseon as she changed course. We seemed to be climbing along the bank of the stream. To our right, crouching mounds, presumably bushes or shrubs huddled like sacks under the snow, briefly appeared.

Why wasn't she simply crossing the stream? Was she looking for a spot where the bank wasn't as steep, for a gentle incline where we wouldn't slip and fall into the snow? She was no longer moving so slowly. I broke rhythm by half a beat, and my feet fell out of the light's range. Everywhere not marked by Inseon's footprints was covered in deep, cold snow. While I heaved my way through, the night eclipsed Inseon's figure so that only a single orb remained, floating up ahead like a tiny spirit.

Now the orb stopped and wavered in mid-air. Was she about to cross over? As I hoisted my legs out of the snow and plunged ahead again, the light resumed its movement. Not away, however.

Slowly, like a candle floating on water, the flame was turning towards me.

⁓

Here, take a look.

Inseon held out something resembling a small, firm fruit.

It looks like an egg, doesn't it?

There was a red speck, like a blood spot on a yolk, on its round, smooth surface.

This swells, the way a bead of blood does around a puncture, she said. Then it starts to open up, like an egg cracking open as it hatches.

So it wasn't a fruit. The tight bulb of rice-coloured petals was dusted with snow that glimmered like sugar granules in the light.

It was a young tree and I shook it as gently as I could, but this one was already loose, Inseon said.

I thought she looked like a young child herself, with her mouth pressed into a tight, sulking pout. And yet her snow-covered hair looked completely grey. I noticed that the palm of her other hand was now holding the bottom of the paper cup. She'd had to push the shrinking candle up inside it.

You're right, she murmured, folding her fingers back over the camellia bud. *We'll lose the light soon.*

We should get back, she added after a pause.

But by now I was asking myself, Do I want to go back? *Where would I even go?* And that was when Inseon lowered herself to the ground, falling on to the snow like silk.

Let's head back in a little bit, she said, looking up at me. I'll make you some juk.

~

The snow on the ground was so soft and pillowy that I felt I might sink infinitely into it. Now a snowbank lay between Inseon and me. I could see only Inseon's face and the candle she had brought to her chest, the rest of her body hidden behind the wall of snow.

The air didn't stir. Each snowflake made its endlessly slow descent, seeming to thread together in mid-air like giant motifs in a lace curtain.

I used to come here with my mum, said Inseon.

I looked out towards where she was staring. All I saw was darkness, a sea of ink. I couldn't tell where the stream ended and the opposite bank began.

The first time we came out here, a storm had swept through the previous day. Mum wanted to see the water. I was maybe ten years old — it wasn't long after my father passed away.

Inseon turned to me. The snowbank, piled up nearly to our shoulders, was like a sheet of silver reflecting the flame back on her, which made it seem as though light were seeping out from within her pale cheeks.

I remember seeing an uprooted tree, its enormous roots exposed, Inseon said. The tree itself wasn't that big, but the roots looked to be three times the size of the crown. I was so struck by them that I stopped short, but my mum had gone ahead without noticing. The weather had cleared up, but the day was still windy. The smell of the wet earth, of fallen flower branches, of grass flattened by the deluge overnight mingled together, prickling my nose. My eyes burned from the sunlight beaming up at me from puddles of rainwater. Like a pair of scissors gliding through a giant sheet of muslin, my mother strode on, cleaving the wind with her body. In that moment, with her blouse and loose trousers billowing out, she loomed as large as a giant to me.

The faintest reverberation of every sound was instantly absorbed by the snow filling the air. I couldn't hear Inseon's breathing. Even the sound of my own breath was swallowed up by the particles of snow.

My mum stopped about here and looked out across the stream, Inseon went on. The water was almost up to the bank and thundering like a cascade. So that's what she meant by going to see the water, I remember thinking as I hurried to catch up. Seeing her hunker down, I followed suit. She heard and turned to me with a smile, reaching out to stroke my cheek. She stroked the back of my head, my shoulders, my back. I remember the feeling of aching love, how it seeped into my skin. Clogging the marrow in my bones and shrivelling my heart . . . That was when I realized. That love was a terrible agony.

◁

After I returned to the island, I sometimes thought back to that day.

More often once my mum in her rapidly deteriorating state began crawling over the doorsill into my room every night, like a child seeking solace.

While I was sleeping, my mum would slip her finger inside my mouth and stroke my face as she wept like a little child. I let her, not having the heart to extract that salty, sticky finger from my mouth. She hugged me with all her strength, so tight I couldn't breathe, couldn't escape and so had no other choice but to hug her back.

The longer her crushing embrace recurred after lights out in that house where no one but us two lived, the harder it became for me to separate my mum's body from my own. Her thin skin, the scant muscles underneath, the lukewarm heat of her body and her disorientation all mingled with mine as one indistinct mass.

Mum didn't only mistake me for her dying little sister. Most times she believed I was her older sister, and at other times a stranger. Some grown-up she didn't know who had come to rescue her. She would grip my wrist so fiercely and say, Save me. Once the sun set, she fell into an even deeper state of confusion and wanted to leave the house. However cold it was outside, however thin the clothes she had on, it didn't *matter. The more I tried to talk her out of it, the more she struggled, and as I tussled with her, feeling her sweaty body against mine, it seemed that I was actually wrestling more than one opponent. Where did her strength come from? After our scuffle, once I had managed to get her to lie down, I would stretch out beside her and shut my eyes, but she was often awake again by then and would shake me when I began to drift off. Because she was afraid of the terrifying confusion that lurked everywhere, mouth wide open and waiting. And afraid she might lose all the connections she had made again the moment she fell asleep. I would beg her to at least let me sleep for half an hour, but she didn't listen. Help me, she said. No sleeping. You have to help me, Inseon-ah.*

We were like a pot of juk bubbling overnight, splattering, overflowing, nearly burning. Help me, save me, she whispered. When at long last she fell asleep, I reached across to touch her face, but at the wetness on her cheeks — it was like she was drowning — I turned away from her. Thinking, How can I? How am I supposed to save you?

The truth is, I wanted to die. It was my only thought for a long while. When a care worker started coming round for four hours a day, I was finally able to go down to the shops, rest my eyes for at least a couple of hours in my truck without interruption and just about cope. But once those hours were up, we had to get on with it on our own: the tussling over her nappies, the having to lift her knees so I could powder her bottom, which made my wrists throb when her legs weren't even heavy. Once she had drifted off, her hands clutching mine, I would bury my head beside her pillow and think, Time has stopped, forever. No one's coming to save us.

Moments of clarity came to her in flashes. Then she was assaulted by memories, which seemed to cut through her like a forged blade. And she would talk. And talk. Like her body had been sliced down the middle by a scalpel, an endless spew of blood-soaked memories. When the lucidity passed, she was even more disorientated. She'd drag me across the floor to hide under the table with her. It seemed that, according to her internal map then, her bedroom corresponded to her childhood home in Hanjinae, my room to the home of the distant cousin, and the span of floor she would crawl to the kitchen, the woods. She didn't loosen her tight grip on me as we hid, and sometimes she surprised me by addressing me by my name. Her chin trembling. All to keep me, who wasn't even born yet, safe.

I observed all this, which was like watching

hundreds of fuses in someone's head humming at once with currents of electricity, then blowing, one by one. At some point, she stopped mistaking me for her sisters. She stopped thinking of me as a grown-up who was there to save her, and she stopped asking for help. She spoke to me less and less, and the words she did say were sporadic and scattered, like islands. Then she stopped saying even yes or no in response, and with that her desires and requests seemed to vanish too. Still, when I placed a peeled mandarin in her hand, she would split it and give me back the bigger half out of lifelong habit, and smile. At which my heart would fall open. I remember wondering if I'd feel that way too towards my child, if I were to have a child.

After this, she started sleeping. As if those endless nights when she'd deprived me of sleep had never been, she was spending two-thirds and later more than three-quarters of the day asleep. In the last month of hospice care, she slept through almost the entire day. It made me think of the sea, but a sea where the high tide lasts forever. Where the water, once it's covered the entire beach, just sits there.

It didn't make any sense. I'd thought when she was gone I would finally get back to my life, but now I realized the bridge back had disappeared. Mum wasn't there to crawl into my room, but I still couldn't sleep. I didn't have to die to escape, but I still wanted to die.

Then early one dawn I came out here.

I'd remembered my promise to you. I wanted to check out the ground I'd said would be good to plant in.

The morning fog was thick that day. The crowns of the bamboo grove, which had got quite tall in ten years, were pretty much all I could make out. But once the half-light lifted and the air began to stir, I could see their entire dim outlines. From there, it wasn't difficult to find the plot where my father's childhood home had been. There was only one parcel of land that had camellia trees instead of a stone fence encircling it, as well as a low stone enclosure built around a barrow in the centre of the yard. Behind the grass-covered foundation stones lay a field full of low-growing broadleaf bamboos, which, in the lingering fog, seemed to ripple out unbounded.

That was the start.

The next day, I began researching Secheon-ri. After visiting the seaside home of the old woman who had witnessed the killings, I read a thesis estimating that thousands of bodies buried at sea here would have been carried away on the currents to Tsushima Island.

That was when I happened across the material about my uncle that my mum had kept in her wardrobe — as I was wondering if I should head to Tsushima next, though I felt at a complete loss because how does one even find washed-up remains, let alone those that sank into the ocean seventy years ago?

And so I changed course, like turning the rudder of a heavy boat. Every day I filled in the gaps in my mum's archive with my finds. Speculating the routes and calculating the times of the ships, buses and trains that would have ferried my mum back and forth between here, Daegu and Gyeongsan back in 1960, and slowly coming to believe that I was losing my mind.

During the day I carved wood in the workshop, and at night I returned to the house and read oral testimonies. With each item, I made sure to cross-check and confirm with the data I had on others who had died. I retraced the sequence of events through US Army records that had been declassified and made accessible after fifty years, the press reports of the time, the lists of prisoners from Jeju who had been incarcerated without trial between 1948 and 1949, and witness accounts and images of the 1950 Bodo League mass killings. At some point, as the materials piled up and began to take on a clearer form, I could feel myself changing. To the point where it seemed nothing one human being did to another could ever shock me again . . . Something deep within my heart had dislodged and the blood that streamed from that gouged space was no longer red or flowing. Instead, a flickering pain throbbed at its jagged surface that only resignation could still . . .

I knew that was where my mum had also found herself. Waking from a nightmare, splashing water on my face and gazing at the mirror, I saw the same persistent quality in my features that had branded hers. What astounded me was the sun's rays, that they returned each day. Steeped in the afterimage of my dreams, I would walk to the woods and find their brutally beautiful light penetrating the foliage and creating thousands upon thousands of light drops. Skeletal forms glimmered over the bright beads. The small body lying on its side with its knees bent in the excavation beneath the landing strip, followed by the bodies of all the people beside it; then a vision of them clothed in flesh and wearing their faces again. Wearing garments stained not in black and white but with fresh blood, lying in the pit with soft curving shoulders and arms and legs that had been alive mere seconds ago.

I had no sense of what my life had been before.

I had to think really hard to remember anything at all. Each time I did, I asked myself where the current was taking me. Who I now was.

It's no coincidence that some thirty thousand people were killed on this island that winter, and another two hundred thousand were murdered on the mainland the next summer. The governing US military ordered that everyone on the island, all roughly three hundred thousand people, be wiped out if that's what it took to stop their communization, and members of the Seocheong, the extreme-right Northwest Youth League, who were from the north and locked and loaded with willingness and resentment, entered the island dressed in police and army uniforms after two weeks of training. Then the coastal blockade and media blackout followed. The murderous impulse to point a gun at an infant's head was not only allowed but rewarded — to the extent that children under the age of ten who were killed in this way numbered one and a half thousand — and shortly after this war broke out, and following the precedent here, if one can call it that when the blood has barely dried, they culled around two hundred thousand people from cities and villages throughout the country, transported them in trucks, incarcerated them, shot them, buried them in mass graves — and then prohibited any and all from claiming and collecting the remains. The war not being over, after all, but merely suspended. As the enemy remains, just over the Armistice Line. As not only shunned and stigmatized families but everyone else kept mum under threat of being branded an enemy sympathizer the moment they opened their mouths. Decades passed in the meantime, decades down in the valleys, the mine, beneath the runway, decades before the mounds of marbles and small skulls shot through with bullet holes were excavated, and still to this day there are bones upon bones that remain buried.

Those children.

Children killed in the name of extermination.

They were on my mind as I left the house that night. It was October, hardly the time for typhoons, but a squall-like gale was sweeping through the woods. Clouds sprinted by, swallowing and disgorging the moon; stars studded the sky and threatened to rain down; the trees writhed as if they were being uprooted. Branches reared and thrashed like wild flames, and the wind ballooning my jacket nearly lifted me off the ground. I took firm, steady steps through the sudden windstorm, and at one point I thought: They're here.

I wasn't afraid. No, I was so happy I could hardly breathe. Rapt in that strange, intense passion — and I couldn't tell if it was excruciating pain or ecstasy — I walked through the biting wind, through the countless gathered who wore bodies spun from wind. It was like I had thousands of transparent needles placed all over my body and they were transfusing me with life. I'm sure I looked mad, perhaps I actually was. In that profound, uncanny euphoria, feeling my heart might rip open, I knew. That now I really could start on our project.

꩜

I waited in the snow.

For Inseon to speak the next words.

No, for her not to.

꩜

The woods behind me were sunk in stillness. From a few kilometres off came the faint sounds of branches buckling.

With her hands wrapped around the candle, Inseon laid her head on the snow and mumbled indistinctly.

This hush — it feels like I've crawled inside cotton wool.

As the wall of snow encircled the flame, our surroundings grew murkier still. The snow-flakes in front of me appeared almost grey. Only the smattering of snow that floated down over Inseon as she lay supine appeared lustrous. I fished out the hood of my duffel from inside my outer coat, pulled it on and lay back in the snow. As I turned my head towards Inseon's voice, a faint glow from the snowbank cast a sombre sheen over my face.

～

It's the strangest thing, Kyungha.

I thought about you every day, and you actually came.

I thought of you so often that I swear sometimes I could almost see you.

Like when you peer inside a dark aquarium.

How if you put your face to the glass and keep looking, you'll eventually see something glimmering inside.

～

Is something looking in on us now? I wondered. Could someone be listening to our conversation?

No, there are only these trees, keeping their silence.

The snow that means to seal us in at the foot of this hill.

⌒

That was when I finally got it, the story my mum had told me when she and I first came here.

She told me that through the fifteen years he was in exile, my father had watched the bank across the stream.

She described how brightly the moon shone on some nights, how the camellia leaves bathed in its glow. How in the early hours, roe deer or the occasional leopard cat would wander down to the middle of the village road, how when heavy rains fell, newly formed brooks and rivulets gushed into this stream bed. She said that was how he saw the half-burned bamboo groves and the camellias grow back, until they were thick and lush again. He would watch from his cell by a night light, and when he closed his eyes, she said he saw small pea-sized sparks floating where the trees had just been.

I didn't believe it, of course.

How seriously my mum took her own story, a story I found implausible even at ten years old, I really don't know. Was it something my father told her at one point? Did they ever come here and look across the stream together?

~

At this, the woman appeared before me. Seen from the back, she was wearing a blouse and a pair of loose-fitting trousers that had swelled with air and looked like wings. This was who had pressed the tip of her pen to the page with such determination and made sure to bend the beginning of each painstaking stroke. *Let's give up. The day of his transfer, we'll consider that the day he died.* This was who had boarded the ferry back to the island alone, musing over these words. Who at long last had stood before the countless shards of broken bones. Who had bowed her head, bent her already bent back lower still, and walked into darkness.

⌣

I don't find her story implausible now, Inseon said.

Or that my father was in prison for fifteen years and also standing right over there.

Or how when I hugged my knees to my chest under my desk, I was also in the pit beneath the runway.

Or how if I kept turning your dream around in my mind, I would see shadows glimmering like fins inside a lightless aquarium.

⌣

Is someone really here with me? I wondered. In the way that light in two different places becomes pinned to a single spot the moment one tries to observe it?

Is that someone you? was my next thought. Are you connected to me now through faintly pulsing threads? Are you peering inside the dark tank, as you try to revive in your hospital room?

∽

Or perhaps the opposite is true. Maybe I'm the one who's dead or dying and keeping watch regardless, still insisting on looking in on this place. From the gloom at the foot of that dry stream. From your icy cold room, where I have returned to lie down after burying Ama.

But how could dying feel this vivid?

Would the flakes of snow seep so coldly into my flesh even in death?

∽

. . . I really shouldn't fall asleep here, Inseon whispered.

Just for a second, though. Let me rest my eyes for just a bit.

She raised an arm over the wall of snow and held out the paper cup. I reached across and took it. The candle stub was shorter than a quarter of a finger now, but the cup itself was warmed through.

Though whether that was from the flame's heat or Inseon's, I couldn't tell.

Holding the cup in front of me, I turned towards where Inseon lay beyond the white divide. In the candle's undeterred blaze, each snow crystal looked to be carrying a kernel of fire. They approached the outer edge of the flame, shuddered as if from the shock of a current, then melted away. A larger snowflake following in their wake reached the flame's bluish heart, dousing it. The wick smoked in its puddle of wax. The sparks sputtered out.

That's OK. I have a light.

I spoke into the darkness. Sitting up, I retrieved the box of matches from my pocket. I felt along its sides to find the rough ignition surface. I struck a match against it. With a burst of sparks, a flame leaped up. The smell of sulphur wafted towards me. I fished the wick out of the melted wax and transferred the flare, but it fizzled out. As I shook out the match, which had burned down to my thumb, the night erased everything again. I couldn't hear the sound of Inseon breathing. I couldn't sense any stirrings of life from the other side of the snowdrift.

Don't disappear on me yet.

Once I've lit this match, I'll reach out and grab your hand, I thought. I'll knock down the snow and crawl over to you, wipe the snow off your cheeks. I'll tear the skin of my finger with my teeth to give you blood.

But if I can't find your hand, that will mean that you've come to and opened your eyes in the hospital.

Where your wounds will be pierced with needles once more. Where blood and electricity will flow together anew.

I inhaled and struck the match. It wouldn't light. I tried a second time, and the match snapped. I held the splintered stick between my thumb and finger and once more scraped its head across the friction surface. Up leaped a flame. Like a blooming heart. Like a pulsing flower bud. Like the wingbeat of an immeasurably small bird.